Angelica's Breath Caught In Her Throat As She Fell From The Stage—And Landed In A Man's Strong Arms.

She stared up at the man who'd saved her. A man she knew by reputation. Paul Sterling—ruthless, cold-blooded corporate shark.

"Thank you for catching me," she said unsteadily.

"My pleasure, angel...."

She glanced up, magnetized by his intense gaze. There was more to this man than his reputation promised. And that *more* was enough to make her pulse pound and her skin tingle.

He lifted her back on the stage, and the auctioneer started the bidding. Many different bids were cast, but the deep voice that cast the *winning* bid—the man she'd be going on three dates with—could belong to only one man. Paul Sterling.

They aren't *real* dates, she reminded herself—but her racing blood didn't seem to notice.

Dear Reader,

Welcome to Silhouette Desire! This month we've created a brand-new lineup of passionate, powerful and provocative love stories just for you.

Begin your reading enjoyment with *Ride the Thunder* by Lindsay McKenna, the September MAN OF THE MONTH and the second book in this beloved author's cross-line series, MORGAN'S MERCENARIES: ULTIMATE RESCUE. An amnesiac husband recovers his memory and returns to his wife and child in *The Secret Baby Bond* by Cindy Gerard, the ninth title in our compelling DYNASTIES: THE CONNELLYS continuity series.

Watch a feisty beauty fall for a wealthy lawman in *The Sheriff & the Amnesiac* by Ryanne Corey. Then meet the next generation of MacAllisters in *Plain Jane MacAllister* by Joan Elliott Pickart, the newest title in THE BABY BET: MacALLISTER'S GIFTS.

A night of passion leads to a marriage of convenience between a gutsy heiress and a macho rodeo cowboy in *Expecting Brand's Baby*, by debut Desire author Emilie Rose. And in Katherine Garbera's new title, *The Tycoon's Lady* falls off the stage into his arms at a bachelorette auction, as part of our popular BRIDAL BID theme promotion.

Savor all six of these sensational new romances from Silhouette Desire today.

Enjoy!

Joan Marlow Golan

Joan Marlow Golan
Senior Editor, Silhouette Desire

Please address questions and book requests to:
Silhouette Reader Service
U.S.: 3010 Walden Ave., P.O. Box 1325, Buffalo, NY 14269
Canadian: P.O. Box 609, Fort Erie, Ont. L2A 5X3

The Tycoon's Lady

KATHERINE GARBERA

Published by Silhouette Books

America's Publisher of Contemporary Romance

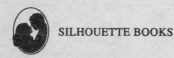 SILHOUETTE BOOKS

ISBN 0-373-76464-2

THE TYCOON'S LADY

Copyright © 2002 by Katherine Garbera

KATHERINE GARBERA

is a transplanted Florida native who is learning to live in Illinois. She's happily married to the man she met in Fantasyland and she spends her days writing, reading and playing with her kids. She is a past recipient of the Georgia Romance Writers Maggie Award.

For John Michael Griffin,
who was lost on September 11,
and for Michael and Michele Griffin, who loved him.

One

'"Let us manage the details of your life while you manage your company,' is their slogan, and anyone who's met Angelica Leone, the cofounder and president, will tell you those details will be in good hands. Gentlemen, may I introduce the next participant in tonight's auction."

Angelica took a deep breath and stepped onstage. She moved slowly as she'd been taught in the private boarding school she'd attended during her formative years. Deportment was one of the areas she'd excelled in. Who would've guessed she'd one day use it to make her living?

She knew that she looked every inch the lady. Knew that the corporate-ladder-climbers were looking her over, searching for a flaw before deciding if she, and by default her company, were worth their money.

Her high-heeled shoes beat the steady tattoo of her steps. She swayed with each movement and focused on the sea of unfamiliar faces beyond the lights at the front of the stage. A few more steps and she'd be at the microphone. Once she was behind the steady wooden barrier she could relax. Public speaking was something she enjoyed.

Distracted by her thoughts, she stumbled over an electrical cord that had been improperly taped and saw her fall from the stage in the kind of slow motion that only movie cameras do well.

She tumbled quickly and had a moment of panic at the thought of landing with her skirt around her hips. There was a sort of stunned silence as even the band stopped playing. Then a murmur of excited voices. She held her breath waiting for her impact with the hard ballroom floor.

Instead she landed solidly in a man's arms. He was strong and warm and smelled faintly of some exotic cologne. His heart beat steadily under her ear. She'd never heard a man's heartbeat before.

Her deceased husband, Roger, had always preferred to keep a certain physical distance between them. For a moment she panicked in the unfamiliar situation and struggled to free herself. The man released her, setting her on her feet.

Her breath caught in her chest as she stared up at the man who'd saved her from the cold hard floor. She knew him by reputation, but they'd never met.

Paul Sterling, a corporate shark that had sent more than one of Angelica's clients looking for a new job.

She owed the last year's profit to him and his drive for success. More than one newly promoted executive had come to her for training in manners and deportment when learning they'd be working under Paul. He demanded perfection from his employees in every aspect of their life.

"Thank you for catching me," she said unsteadily.

"My pleasure, Angel," he said. The words washed over her like a warm breeze on a cool spring day. It had been a long time since a man had stirred more than her business interest.

She glanced up, magnetized by his intense gaze. There was more to this man than his reputation promised. And that *more* was enough to make her pulse pound and her skin tingle. She couldn't tear her gaze away. He wasn't the cold-blooded monster his reputation painted him to be. *Why did that worry her?*

"It's Angelica. Angelica Leone."

"Paul Sterling," he said.

"I know." She spoke before she'd thought, a major fault of hers that had landed her in hot water more than once.

He raised one eyebrow in response but Angelica suddenly became aware of all the people around them. Her face felt hot. Not exactly the image she hoped to gain for her company. She tried to figure out how to get back on the stage, and her rescuer lifted her to the platform with little difficulty.

Two stage technicians rushed out and taped the cord down. She refused to glance at Paul again, though she knew she owed him a debt of gratitude. Would cigars be sufficient? Or did saving someone from an embarrassing situation deserve something more? Something with a monogram. She'd have to check her Emily Post when she got home.

She made it to the podium and clutched it as if it was a lifesaver and she was the last survivor on a sinking ship. "Situations just like that one are what we're equipped to teach you to handle. But more importantly, we're ready to show you how to navigate the more familiar waters of corporate socializing. Tonight you will be bidding on our Silver Bells Package, which includes domestic management of your house for three months and a partner at three corporate functions."

She smiled at the emcee and he started the bidding. She was conscious of many different bids being cast, but the deepest voice that had the winning bid could belong to only one man—Paul Sterling. Angelica knew that a box of cigars was never going to satisfy him.

The one man in the room who'd made her remember she was a woman was the same man she'd just agreed to spend three dates with. They aren't real dates, she reminded herself, but her racing blood didn't seem to notice.

*   *   *

Paul carried two glasses of champagne across the ballroom to Angelica Leone. He had come to the auction tonight more out of curiosity than any other reason and he was glad he'd done so. Though he'd lived in Orlando for the last ten years he'd never attended the annual event.

He was finally at a place in his life where he could mingle socially and not miss the time away from his desk. At last the end was in sight. He was about to become the youngest CEO in the history of Tarron Enterprises.

He wouldn't have to spend the next few weeks finding an eligible young woman and courting her, as much as dating today could be called courting, now that he had a ''corporate wife'' to attend the annual board of directors meeting with him.

He'd always been a loner by nature and necessity but recently his boss had been dropping hints about a balanced life. Paul knew the solution was to marry someone who was like-minded but his one glimpse of marriage had left a sour taste in his mouth. The fact that it had been his parents' wasn't something he liked to examine too closely. *Especially not tonight.*

He'd heard a lot about Corporate Spouses but nothing about its lovely owner. The dark-haired beauty stirred a primitive response in him. He was used to ignoring those impulses. He'd survived his long climb to the top by doing just that. Why then was he tempted to find a very intimate way to work her out of his system?

At this point the singles scene was more of a chore than a game. Though sometimes he wished for a companion, he knew marriage wasn't for him. The past had taught him that women didn't understand his obsession with his job and working was the only thing that he could count on.

This "corporate wife" thing might be just what he needed. Certainly it would be helpful to have someone intelligent and well mannered by his side. And judging from her reputation she was all of that. But there were hidden layers beneath her surface which aroused his curiosity.

"Champagne?" he asked, finding her alone when the couple she'd been talking to drifted off to the dance floor.

"I should be bringing you a drink. Thanks again for catching me." She took the flute from his hand and held her glass up for a toast.

Her red dress clung to her curves in a subtle way that teased him with what it revealed and hid. She reminded him of dark passions and hidden longings. She was understated and elegant but the way she'd moved on stage promised something more. The energy in her voice when she'd spoken about her company bespoke hidden depths.

"To fate," Paul said. They clinked their glasses and he noticed that Angelica's eyes held his the entire time.

She had large brown eyes. They seemed to dominate her face and promised the secrets to her soul, but at a very high price. Paul was used to paying top dollar for whatever he wanted. Cost didn't bother him when he was investing money. Emotions—he didn't invest those easily.

"To heroes," she said, and took a tentative sip.

"You'd be better to drink to fate because I'm no hero."

"Well, tonight you were mine and I appreciated it."

"It was nothing. I'd gladly do it again."

She looked away as if uncomfortable and he took a sip of his drink to give himself time to think. Silence grew between them. All the suave sophistication he'd thought he'd cultivated was gone in an instant. He had nothing to say.

Falling back on the one thing that never failed him, he brought up business.

A jazz trio started to play and couples slowly filled the small dance floor. For a moment Paul thought of all he'd given up in his quest to become the best at what he did. But he ignored the pang, knowing that those things wouldn't make him happy the way his career did.

He glanced at Angelica and she, too, stared at the couples as if she wished she was on the dance floor. Well, he wasn't asking her to dance. Theirs was to be a business relationship and he meant for it to stay that way.

"Explain the particulars of the package I purchased to me," he blurted out.

"It's our Silver Bells Package, which includes three months of domestic management and a specified number of dates, in your case three. We can talk specifics Monday morning if you'd like.''

''Would 10:30 be okay?'' he asked.

''Sure,'' she answered.

Three dates sounded like too many forced encounters and at the same time seemed like too few. She enchanted him with her hourglass figure and midnight hair. Her mind was sharp and he knew she revealed little of what she really felt. When she'd fallen off the stage, she'd never looked ruffled. She'd been prepared to handle whatever happened.

Paul had the same self-confidence that came from knowing you could manage anything and he liked that about Angelica. In fact, he plain liked too much about her.

''Tell me more about your business. Is it more than dates for receptions?'' he asked.

''Yes. We serve as a fill-in at corporate functions. So if your company had bought a table here tonight and everyone was bringing a spouse and yours was unavailable, we'd fill in.''

''Has anyone tried to cross that line and make the date more real that it is?'' he asked, knowing he'd be tempted to. But women like Angelica deserved more than he had to give.

His motto was a smart man knew his limits. Paul was careful to stay within his. He was your guy for corporate takeovers and labor management. He was your guy for a winning partner at basketball. But he wasn't your guy if you were a woman looking for the long haul.

And though he knew he'd just met Angelica, she had the look of a woman who'd expect more from a man than a few nights of pleasure in his bed. *Remember that.*

"Not with me," she said.

He believed it. There was a core of strength in her that warned men she wasn't going to play any of the games they might want to play. It probably came from the self-confidence he'd admired earlier, but it didn't make it any easier to deal with her.

The band switched to a raucous swing number that had been made popular by the old Stray Cats lead singer Brian Setzer and enticed the younger crowd onto the floor and a couple of old-timers who were by far the best dancers out there. Angelica tapped her foot as she watched the couples moving across the floor.

"I took swing lessons last year," she said out of the blue.

He wanted to smile at her. She reminded him of his sister before life had burned all of the excitement out of her. That precious time when life still seemed like happily-ever-after glowed in Angelica's eyes and for a minute…just a minute, he wished he was the guy to give it to her. But he lived in a concrete real world and knew happily-ever-after was only a myth.

"I've never learned."

"We offer lessons at Corporate Spouses. I can toss them in if you're interested."

"No, thanks. I don't like to waste time."

She stared at him as if he were a merger gone sour. "Socializing is an important part of the business world."

"I can socialize without dancing."

"What about fun?" she asked.

"What about it? Business and fun don't mix."

"They can," she said.

"Not for everyone."

He admired her dedication to her company. He thought about that dedication. Told himself that his interest in her was purely as one executive to another. But his gut told him something different.

The swing song ended and they both applauded the band and the couples. A tall African-American woman dressed in a slim-fitting dress joined the trio. The first strains of a Lena Horne standard filled the air. The soloist had a voice that rivaled Lena's.

Paul tossed back the remainder of his champagne and gave his glass to a passing waiter. Angelica set hers on the tray as well though he noticed her glass was still half-full.

"Will you dance with me?" she asked.

Damn. He shouldn't. Say no.

"Sure."

He wasn't certain where the word had come from. True he'd been dying to get her back in his arms since he'd set her down earlier, but he didn't dance at business socials. It was like being a new colorful fish in a tankful of dull brown guppies. But he couldn't resist the chance to hold her.

"Are you positive? There's no way this can be considered business."

"Yes, it can, Angel. It's your business."

"Is that the only thing in your life?" she asked.

The heavy pumping of his blood said that it used to be. But if he wanted to have even half a chance at keeping things between them tame, he needed to remember she was a business partner...an employee, if you will.

He tugged her into his arms and realized that he was doomed, because none of his employees had ever given him an erection before.

Angelica tried to keep a respectable distance between them but it was a struggle. His shoulders felt large and solid under her touch, just right for resting her head. He held her with a surety that promised he'd easily guide her through the dance and whatever troubles life offered. And that made her uncomfortable.

By circumstance she'd always shouldered her own burdens and though sometimes deep in the night she wished for someone masculine to lean on, in reality she knew that she could only depend on herself. That thought gave her the willpower she needed to resist her attraction to him.

"I love this song," she said. Small talk was her forte usually. She'd been known to mingle in a crowd filled with the most powerful men and women in the city and never lose her cool. Yet here she was losing her composure on the dance floor with just one man.

Except he didn't feel like just *one man* to her. He felt like *the man*. The only one that she'd ever felt quite right dancing with since her wedding night seven years ago. It was definitely time for her to start dating again when she was attracted to a client.

Paul murmured something unintelligible. Angelica wasn't sure what that meant. Sometimes Rand Pearson, her partner in Corporate Spouses, did that but usually it was during a sporting event.

"Don't like jazz?" she asked. Come on, she thought. The true skill of small talk was finding something the other person wanted to talk about. Usually it was themselves. Nervously, she tucked a strand of hair behind her ear.

Paul Sterling had enough ego for three men, you could see it in the way he moved. It would be easier if he was vain. But their interaction so far had showed he was self-confident, but didn't think he was a god.

"I'm not a big fan of this type of music. Give me some straightforward rock and roll and I'm a happy guy."

"Why rock?"

"There's just something about songs that talk about women and sex that appeal to me."

She flushed and pretended she hadn't noticed that there was something sexual in his eyes. Something purely masculine gleamed there, and for the first time since she'd started her business six years ago she was uncomfortable in a social setting.

"Um…well. I've always liked jazz."

"You would," he said, running his hand down her spine.

A shiver followed his touch, spreading throughout her body, pooling in her center. "Why?"

His eyes narrowed. "Because it's subtle and mysterious and essentially that's what women are."

Back away, she thought. Thank him for dancing with you and move away from him before you get burned by the heat in his touch.

Instead of listening to her inner voice, she said, "Oh, my. Have we been burned in the past?"

"Isn't that a little personal for a first dance?"

Embarrassed, she looked away. They circled the floor once more and Angelica decided to try again.

"This is a perfect example of what Corporate Spouses provides. You'd be surprised how many young people climb the ladder at work only to realize they don't have the skills necessary to do the socializing their job requires," she said, trying to ignore the warm pulsing of her skin where he touched the small of her back.

The smile he gave her wasn't reassuring and she knew she'd crossed a line earlier but she'd felt goaded. He was a challenge to her. Mr.-No-Fun made her want to prove to him that sometimes having fun was as important as being successful. Something she knew he didn't believe.

"I have no doubt you'd be the perfect accessory

in a business setting.'' His voice changed little in tone, but there was a glint in his eyes that made her wish she knew him better. She couldn't tell if he was serious or not. And if he was, she dreaded the next three months.

It had taken her a long time to find her footing alone in the world and Corporate Spouses gave her exactly what she needed. Companionship at night, a challenge during the day. She wasn't about to let lust mess that up.

''You make me sound like a Rolex,'' she said. She'd never owned one. Though she had to dress the part of a wealthy woman in her business life, at home she owned a cheap generic watch. It seemed a little insane to her to pay a lot of money for something that performed the same function as its cheaper sister.

''In essence you will be.''

''You're joking, right?'' Damn, what was with her tonight? She'd learned long ago to guard her tongue, but it seemed that Paul's touch made her forget that she was only making small talk. She should be letting him carry the conversation and not leading him on.

''No. Most relationships are like buying an expensive piece of jewelry or a European driving machine. There has to be a lot of thought given to the money you're spending and the appropriateness of what you've purchased.''

Angelica couldn't believe her ears. She wanted to be indignant, but he wasn't being insulting. Just stating the way he looked at the world. She almost wished she believed as he did. It would have been a great shield to protect herself from the pain of losing her husband so young. Did Paul Sterling have a similar tragedy in his past?

"But a date shouldn't be all business," she said.

"In our case it is," he said smoothly.

He was quick on his feet. She liked that in a man. "Yes, but you were talking generally."

"I only meant that with you the vetting had been done. You're a known commodity in a social situation."

She suddenly felt like the Hope Diamond, viewed by many and touched by none. "Kind of like a Rolex. You know that I'll look nice and function well."

"Exactly," he said.

"I wouldn't share that attitude with your dates," she said wryly.

"I don't."

She realized then that Paul had handed her an effective barrier to use against the attraction she felt for him. This man, who viewed people as possessions, was not a man she wanted to spend more than the required amount of time with.

"Why did you share it with me?"

He maneuvered them into a quiet secluded corner. He still held her loosely, but the tone of his embrace had changed. He looked down at her; masculine intent gleamed in his eyes. With a hand under her chin, he tipped her face up to his.

"Do you really want to know?" he asked.

No, but she didn't back down from challenges. "Yes."

"I liked the feel of you in my arms earlier."

"Oh."

"And I intend to have you there again."

Oh my God, she thought. She wouldn't say anything out loud again. She told herself to walk away. To turn her head a mere two inches left and relieve her skin of his warm callused finger. But she didn't.

His eyes held her captive but she knew it wasn't against her will. He'd sparked some deep primal response in her from the moment she'd tumbled into his arms. No matter how dangerous the attraction might be, a part of her wanted to explore it. But not with this man.

"I'm curious too, but we can never have more than a business relationship."

She started to walk away and barely heard his response, but the words echoed for a long time in her mind.

"I'll be damned."

It wasn't the words that lingered in her head. It was the conviction with which he said them that had her worried.

Two

Angelica kicked the stubborn tire and felt the back of her eyes burn as pain shot up her leg. A flat tire was just what she needed. She'd left the hotel ballroom with the applause of womankind in her ears, her feminine strength and power at their pinnacle. And now as she struggled with the lug-nut wrench, trying desperately to free her punctured tire, she knew she'd have to rely on a man to get it off.

That angered her because she liked being self-reliant. She was going to have to call the mechanic first thing in the morning and get a different wrench for the car. One that she could use easily. She glanced up and down the deserted road. At least it was a well-lit side street.

She hunted in her evening bag for her cellular

phone and dialed the auto club. As usual they were busy, but promised to have someone to her in the next hour. The wind kicked up and Angelica decided to wait in her car. It was chilly in Florida in February. Especially this close to the witching hour.

She started to dial Rand's number. He lived only five minutes from here, and although Rand would change the tire for her she didn't want to call her partner. She didn't want him to know there was something she couldn't do. Her reputation was on the line.

A sleek Mercedes roadster pulled alongside her and stopped in front of her car. Fight-or-flight impulses ran through her body, making her tingle. She fumbled for the door to her car, knowing she'd feel safer with a barrier between her and whoever drove the car.

Then the door opened and Paul Sterling emerged from his car. As he walked toward her, Angelica took her finger off the emergency button on her phone and relaxed a little bit. She'd rather have called Rand than have to deal with Paul Sterling now. Why hadn't she just driven on despite the flat?

"I thought that was you," he said carefully. Then examining the doughnut tire and jack on the road, asked, "Flat tire?"

"Yes. I can change one myself but these nuts are too tight."

"Want some help?" he offered.

No, she thought. She wanted to be able to do this on her own but she wanted to be home more. "Yes, please. I called the auto club. It could take an hour for someone to get here.''

''I can do it in no time. I worked my way through high school in an auto shop.''

He didn't look like the blue-collar type. As he changed the tire it became apparent he was very proficient at it. She knew she should say something to him but she only stood there watching him work.

She wanted to ask him about his past. Why had he worked in an auto shop? She needed some distance from this man who reawakened too many impulses she'd thought were gone forever.

This was twice he'd rescued her, and she knew she'd have to do more than send him the monogrammed tie she'd been planning as a thanks for catching her. Maybe some imported cigars or an engraved card case.

He finished with the tire and stored the flat and the tools in her trunk.

''Thank you, Paul. I don't usually need to be rescued twice in the same evening.''

''It was my pleasure. But don't start thinking I'm a white knight.''

''What are you?''

''Not a hero. Just a guy who happened to be in the right place at the right time.''

''I don't believe that at all,'' she said.

''Don't read too much into my actions. I just can't stand to see a woman in jeopardy.''

''Why?'' she asked. Maybe it was the moon and

stars or the quiet of the night but she wanted to know more about him.

"Because I know what life does to a woman who doesn't have a man to lean on."

"It makes her strong," Angelica said. That exact process was responsible for the woman she was today. She'd been married young and had looked forward to a life of letting her husband make all the decisions. She'd have been happy in that life but she'd never have been fulfilled, she realized. It was only when he'd died on their honeymoon, leaving her alone, that she'd truly discovered herself and what she was capable of.

"For some women. But it makes others bitter and leaves them lonely."

"The same can be said of men."

"It's different for men. We're used to being alone but women aren't."

"Who do you know who is like that?" she asked. Damn, she needed to learn to stop asking personal questions. Here was a man she wanted to keep her distance from. Why then did she keep inviting him closer?

"No one who's living," he said quietly. There was a coldness to his words that reminded her they were standing outside on a winter's night. She wanted to comfort him but had the feeling he wouldn't welcome her touch. Instead she fumbled in her pocket for her keys, shivering against the breeze.

Paul pulled her collar up around her face. The

touch of his fingers against her skin sent another shiver through her but it was of a different nature.

"You better get home before you catch a chill. Want me to follow you?"

"No. I'll be fine."

He nodded and walked back to his car. She climbed carefully into her car and eased onto the street. She saw his lights in her rearview mirror all the way home and though she knew it shouldn't, they gave her a sense of security.

Paul Sterling might not believe he was a hero but his instincts and actions made him one. Why did he fight that side of himself?

When she pulled into her development, he made a U-turn and headed back the other way. She was more touched than she should be that he'd seen her safely home. The cold-blooded corporate shark was really a man of refinement and manners. Underneath his smooth professional surface beat the wounded heart of a good man.

As she pulled into her driveway, Angelica reminded herself that she was out of the business of rescuing wounded warriors. She repeated the words as she entered her house, turned on the heat and readied herself for bed. But somehow her subconscious didn't get the message, because the last image she saw as she drifted to sleep was Paul Sterling.

Paul's office overlooked downtown Orlando. The skyline was crisp and clean; no billowing clouds of pollution from local factories filled the air. Orlando was a cow town that owed its development to the tourism industry. Some of the small-town charm lingered in the big city it had become.

There was a discreet knock on his door and he pivoted from the window. Corrine Martin, his secretary, stood in the doorway. She had been with him for the last three years. She was young, smart and ambitious. He knew she'd go far. The only thing keeping her in his outer office was an insane amount of money and the respect he gave her.

"Angelica Leone, your ten-thirty appointment, is here."

"Send her in," he said, sitting down behind his desk. The desk was large and impressive, befitting the man who would one day run Tarron, and Paul loved it. His entire office was set up to give him the home-court advantage and today he needed that edge more than ever.

Angelica walked into the room looking competent and chic. Her suit was all business yet still managed to look feminine. The skirt ended just above her knees. Her legs were long and lean. Staring at them, he wondered what they'd feel like wrapped around his hips. Would her skin be as soft there as it had been on her hand?

He gestured toward one of the guest chairs and she sank gracefully into it. She'd tamed her hair into a chignon and if he hadn't seen the dark masses flowing around her shoulders, he might have preferred this look on her. But all the hairstyle did this morning was make him want to pull out the pins and bury his hands in it.

She reached into her large black bag and pulled out a wrapped present that totally threw him off track. He'd been prepared for a business meeting. Friday night had proven she wanted nothing from him but what he'd bought at the auction.

But her eyes, hair and body had convinced his primal instincts that he wanted more. He wouldn't be content until he had her in his bed. He knew that wasn't what she was here for. He needed to stop reacting to her and start thinking of her as a business associate he wanted to win over.

"Thanks again for rescuing me Friday night," she said, placing the present on his desk.

Pulling the package closer to him, he toyed with the dark-maroon ribbon. There was a card attached and a neat delicate hand had written his name in script. Was this her handwriting? Damn, he hated it when someone did something unexpected.

He pushed the package aside. His focus wouldn't be deterred. He knew exactly where Angelica Leone was going to fit in his life and that spot didn't involve the warm feelings currently pulsing around the pit of his stomach.

"The first service I'll need from you is to be my hostess at a party for my staff."

She pulled her planner from her bag and started taking notes. "How many people?"

"About fifty with spouses." He wondered what she'd gotten him. It had been a long time since anyone not related to him had given him a gift. In fact, only his older sister, Layne, had ever given him a gift. Occasionally he got a bottle of wine or a gift basket from a colleague or client. Maybe that's what this was.

"What date are you targeting for your get-together?" she asked, her eyes straying to the package.

"The last weekend in March." Did she want him to open it? It wasn't the right shape to be a bottle of wine.

She jotted a few more notes on her pad. "Barely four weeks. That'll be tight depending on what venue you want. But I know a caterer who will squeeze you in."

"Good. I don't want a bunch of trendy food that no one can identify. I push my staff hard during the year and this has to be a party they remember."

"Why are you doing it now instead of at year-end?"

"I was hired by Tarron on March 29 and I like to celebrate my company anniversary with the people who are responsible for my success."

She smiled at him and it went straight to his groin. He'd been in a state of semi-arousal since he'd left her last night. He still felt the cool touch of her fingers on his cheek and wanted more than anything else to feel that touch elsewhere on his body.

"We better increase the head count to sixty," he said. "I'm going to invite my boss and some of the board members as well."

"Okay. Do you give your staff thank-you gifts?"
She crossed her legs, and her skirt, that slim respectable garment, slid two inches up her thigh. Her leg was lean and though covered in nylon hose, his fingers tingled with the need to caress her. He had to clench his hands and stare at his desk for a minute before he could look at her again.

Damn, she'd asked a question. What was it? Images of her sitting in front of him on his desk while he slid his hands up her sweet legs filled his mind. He heard her voice calling his name and moaning as ecstasy overcame her.

"Paul?"

"Yes?"

"Gifts for your staff?"

"I've never given them anything but I'd like to this year. What do you suggest?"

Thank God he was sitting behind his desk or he'd have a lot of explaining to do. He'd never reacted to a woman this quickly before. Had certainly never had a fantasy about one when she was sitting in his office in a business meeting. Maybe it was time he really started dating or had a one-night stand. Even as the thought entered his mind he knew he wouldn't be satisfied with any woman save Angelica.

"Let me look into it and I'll send some ideas to you by tomorrow afternoon."

"Good. One more thing, I want to have the party on my yacht. Will your caterer be able to work in the small galley?"

Her face turned ashen and she dropped her pencil. "Your yacht?"

"Yes, are you okay?"

"I'm fine," she said, tucking a nonexistent strand of hair behind her ear.

But he could tell she wasn't. All thoughts of lust left him and he wanted to comfort her instead. Something he'd never wanted to do in the past, but now he could barely control the impulse to open his arms and let her rest against him.

"Do you have a problem with the yacht?" he asked.

"Of course not, it sounds like a lovely idea. What about having it at a yacht club? You'd still have the lovely beach views but you wouldn't be on the water."

"I'm set on the yacht."

"Not everyone is comfortable on the water."

Was Angelica one of those people? "My staff is. I took them out on it last year when I first purchased it."

"Oh."

"Do you have a problem with the yacht, Angelica?"

She glanced up at him. "No, not the yacht."

"Good, then it's all settled." But he had a feeling it was far from settled. As she put her planner away and leaned back in her chair, he knew that he was right.

"Now that business is taken care of... Will you open my present?"

He swallowed and reached for the package. He felt oddly vulnerable as he peeled the ribbon away and he resented Angelica for making him feel that way. He'd always been strong and in control in all of his relationships.

Angelica focused on Paul opening her gift. She'd decided on a silk tie before she went to the store but her final selection wasn't as impersonal as she'd hoped. Which bothered her because it proved that she wasn't as immune to Paul as she'd like to be.

Not that the gift was her first clue. Her sleep the last two nights had been plagued with dreams of him and her. Lena Horne sang about throwing love away while they danced in the rain. She'd almost canceled their appointment this morning but she knew better than to give ground.

The success she'd made of Corporate Spouses came because she was willing to go to the edge for her clients. This was the first time she'd gone to such a deeply emotional one. And she didn't like it.

The last man who'd tempted her like this had been Roger. And she wanted to prove to herself that she'd learned something.

That she wouldn't fall for a man with dark brooding eyes that made her feel alive from the top of her head to the tips of her toes. Even though just thinking about being on the water again reminded her of Roger, attraction ran through her veins, forcing her to admit she was alive. Watching Paul hesitate in unwrapping his gift gave her something to concentrate on.

"I wish you hadn't done this," he said. And his face confirmed that he was uncomfortable.

"You saved me—twice. I wouldn't have felt right without giving you something."

A blush burned her cheeks as he stared at her. She wasn't used to bringing a man's attention to her on an intimate level, and there was something very intimate in Paul's gaze.

"I'm not a gracious receiver," he said.

What did that mean? She wanted to ask but knew better. She warned herself to just sit tight and let him open the gift. Then get out of there—quick.

"Why not?" she asked, then wanted to look around for her evil twin.

He stopped messing with the package. "If I tell you it'll just add to the black mark next to my name."

"You're my hero, you don't have a black mark." He *was* her hero. She'd been alone for so long that she'd taken for granted that she'd always have to do everything herself.

"I am the man who said wives and Rolexes should involve the same amount of attention." There was something flirty in his eyes.

Her heart beat a little faster as she pulled out her planner. Don't flirt, she repeated to herself but the temptation was irresistible. "I'd forgotten about that. Let me add that to my notes... Oh, you better give me back the gift."

He arched one eyebrow at her, leaning across his desk. "Are you always a smart-ass?"

"Usually only when I'm dealing with one. Come on, tell me why you don't like to receive."

"It's not a matter of liking. I just don't have a lot of practice at it."

"I find that hard to believe. Your position alone would garner you gifts."

"That's different. I work hard here and those things are a direct result of my efforts. But this isn't."

"It's personal."

"Yeah, *personal.*"

He was quiet as he opened the box and read the card she'd laid on the tie. The neck garment was by the same designer as the suit he'd been wearing the night of the auction. She doubted he'd notice.

"I thought we agreed I was no one's white knight."

She shrugged, afraid to open her mouth and say something she'd regret. Her card had been simple— *Thanks for being my Rhett Butler.*

He pulled the tie from the box and the money clip fell free. *Guard what you hold most dear* was inscribed on the clip. She knew that the Moola Clip was talking about cold hard currency, but she'd meant something deeper and if Paul was half the man she believed him to be, he'd know that.

"Thank you," he said.

She couldn't read him, which made her vulnerable. Angelica had spent all of her adult life proving she wasn't fragile. "Is it okay?"

"Yeah, I like it."

She had the feeling he really did. Silence grew between them and the intense look in his eyes reminded her that he was man to her woman. Reminded her of the fit and feel of his body against hers on the dance floor the other night. Reminded her that she'd been on her own too long and there was a very good reason why people kept getting married.

"I'm never sure what to buy for men. Well, I only buy for one man other than my dad, that's my partner, Rand, and that's different because—"

"It's one of the most thoughtful gifts I've ever received," he said. Standing, he came around his desk and stood before her.

"I've always found men somewhat difficult to buy for. You all think differently than we do."

"No kidding."

She wrinkled her nose at him. "Well, I guess I'll be on my way. Are you sure I can't convince you to have the party in a clubhouse or banquet room?"

"No. But I might consider a reception room at the yacht club if you tell me why you're so adamant about avoiding the yacht."

"I'm not."

"Whatever you say."

"It's just that some people have a thing about water."

"You mentioned that earlier. Are you one of those people?"

"Yes."

"Would it be better for you if we stayed anchored in the marina?"

"No," she said carefully.

"Can you swim?" he asked.

"Yes," she said. She was a good swimmer, scuba diver and water-skier, but she hadn't been able to go near the ocean or any of the lakes that dotted the Florida landscape since her husband had died on their honeymoon. But she wasn't going to share any details of her past with Paul Sterling. His dark perceptive gaze already saw too much of what she'd rather hide.

Three

———

Paul knew he should return to his position of security behind the desk but those big brown eyes of hers had drawn him across the room. He wanted to protect her...or ravish her. To kiss those soft pink lips until whatever made her sad was a very distant memory. Maybe it was because she thought he was a white knight that he felt compelled to be one.

But he knew that he'd only be playacting. He'd been leaning toward her and now he pulled back. Physical desire was one thing, but he couldn't mix it with emotion. Lust surged through him as he breathed deeply. Her scent was lightly floral and uniquely feminine. It called all of his primal instincts to the fore.

Damn, he needed a real date more than he'd

thought. He was in the office, for Christ's sake, not in a bar. He slid back onto his desk and propped one ankle on his knee.

"Why don't you want to go out on the boat?" he asked again. Talk, he thought. Distract me from your lips. They can't possibly be as soft and as sweet as they look.

She bit her lip. And he groaned to himself, wanting to be the one tasting that tempting flesh.

"It's too personal."

"This from the woman who asked me about my love life on the dance floor."

She tilted her head. A tendril of hair escaped the sleek pins holding it up. It curled invitingly against her neck. The contrast of creamy skin and dark luxuriant hair wasn't lost on him. He had to clench his hands to keep from finding out if that tendril would curl around his finger.

"I believe you declined to answer."

She had him and he had a feeling she didn't even know it. She'd stayed longer in his office than anyone else ever had. He had a strict fifteen-minute policy that he usually enforced to keep himself on schedule and to make sure his meetings weren't a waste of time. But he didn't think the thirty minutes he'd spent with Angelica was squandered. Later, he knew, he'd regret giving her more than fifteen minutes.

"You're right. This is none of my business. It's just that you seemed...I don't know...upset."

She said nothing.

He knew he should let it go, but he couldn't. So he thought about it for a minute and decided the key to Angelica was through the emotions he read in her eyes. "You're the one who said I was a white knight. I knew I wasn't."

He stood up and walked around the desk. Her hand on his wrist stopped him. He glanced down at her, but she wasn't looking at him. Victory rushed through him. Getting people to spill their secrets was a skill he'd always possessed.

He never used it to hurt anyone. You needed to see what was going on inside someone before you knew what they really wanted. Life had taught him that once someone bared their soul they expected you to do the same and Paul refused to be that vulnerable.

Her hand on his felt small and fragile, but she held him with strength. She really did make him feel like a warrior of old. Not a man in polished armor, but a battered and weary man in pelts who could defend her from whatever life threw at her.

He also recognized that Angelica had a rock-hard core underneath her neat and pretty exterior. She'd carved a place for herself in the business world where there was a need. It took savvy to do that. He admired her.

He understood that kind of strength because he was the same inside. He knew the kind of trials one had to endure to become that solid. Trial by fire tempered a person like the finest steel. He wondered what in her past had shaped her.

But she was a business associate not a woman he was dating and he knew better than to mix business and pleasure. Still, a part of him thought she'd make the perfect corporate wife. Not just because she'd been successfully playing the part for years, but because they seemed to get along well. And frankly, he wanted her in his bed.

He'd never been able to sleep around casually. He'd had one one-night stand when he was nineteen and it had left him with a bad taste in his mouth. He never wanted to wake up with a stranger again. Besides, his career was his life and dating took too much time and effort.

"Angel, I just want to know why your eyes are misty."

She shrank back from him, carefully pulling herself away and replacing the shield she'd worn when she'd entered the room. All traces of sadness left her face even though an aura of vulnerability lingered around her. If he hadn't spent his formative years with a woman with the same aura he wouldn't have recognized it.

"I didn't know it showed."

"Tell me," he said softly. Knowing from his mother that women liked to talk about the things that hurt them the most deeply.

"My husband was killed on the water during our honeymoon."

Jesus. No wonder she didn't want to go on the water. "We can have the party elsewhere."

"No. This is my year to take."

"I don't understand."

"I'm taking back my life."

He nodded. He knew what it was like to let fears control you. He wasn't brave enough to risk trusting another person with his emotions. He'd seen the devastation that had brought. He understood the need to take back your life. Hadn't that been what he'd started out to do when he entered the corporate world?

He didn't like to dwell on his own shortcomings, so he focused instead on Angelica. "Then why'd you argue to move the venue."

"I didn't say the process was easy."

He realized that she wasn't committed to leaving the risk-free zone. He appreciated that she was trying. "No, it's not. How'd your husband die?"

"We were water skiing and he did this three-and-a-half twist off the ramp, but the momentum wasn't right. He hit the ramp on his descent. The driver stopped after less than a minute. But it was too late. They said he was killed immediately."

"How old were you?"

"Twenty-one."

Without really thinking, he knelt beside her and put his arm around her and pulled her close. She laid her head on his shoulder. She nestled so trustingly in his arms that he knew he shouldn't betray that. Her curves held so close had a distinct effect on him. When she tilted her head back, he lowered his and brushed his lips over her mouth.

* * *

Trouble, Angelica knew, came often from the corners you least expected it from. She'd known Paul was no good for her from the moment he'd caught her in his arms in the crowded ballroom. Though he'd offered her safety, his body had promised temptation. And she'd always been able to resist temptation. Why now was it so hard?

The pressure of his lips against her own tempted her and for once she gave in to the impulse. Though his demeanor said let me comfort you, his body language said something else entirely. She was woman enough to want to listen to what his body had to say.

As their lips met, Angelica couldn't help opening her mouth and inviting him closer. He took the invitation and more ground than she'd intended to give him. As soon as his tongue thrust past the barrier of her teeth, she forgot about ground and walls and how badly men could hurt you without even trying.

Paul cradled her head in his hands, controlling the overtone of the embrace. He dropped light kisses on her mouth and face. She kept her eyes wide open, not wanting to miss one nuance. Paul's eyes, which were incredibly light, watched her carefully.

She felt feminine and fragile even though she wasn't. She felt young and new to passion though she'd experienced a man's kisses before. She felt alive in a way that her business never made her feel. The walls she'd built carefully to protect her heart began to crumble.

No man had held her so tenderly since her husband had slipped from her embrace into a watery grave. And that scared her. She pulled back.

"A white knight for the weekend and already I want to tarnish my armor," Paul said. Their embrace clearly catching him as unaware as it had her.

There was a self-critical part of Paul Sterling that Angelica didn't like. He was a good man with a reputation for fair play. Why then was he the only one who couldn't see it?

"A simple kiss won't bring you ruin." *Please God let that be true.*

She'd forgotten how intimate it was to be exchanging breath with someone. She'd forgotten how the mind shut down and instincts took over. She'd forgotten how it felt to be a woman and now awakened, she reveled in it.

"How little you know, Angel."

His breath whistled through his teeth as he pulled back. But Angelica knew that this embrace wouldn't happen again and didn't want it to stop. She closed her eyes so her vulnerability wouldn't be seen by this man who'd touched places she'd tried to shut away. He saw through her anyway. And though she couldn't see him she could feel him. The humid touch of his mouth on her neck, the exhalation of his breath against her ear, the caress of his hands along her back.

She cupped the back of his head and neck, urging his face toward hers. His heat surrounded her and then his arms did. She closed her eyes as his lips touched hers once more, pressing this moment into the scrapbook in her mind to keep forever.

Her torso brushed against his chest. He was rock solid, but then she'd known he was muscular. He'd caught her without sign of stress the night of the auction. She couldn't think of one other man who'd ever been there when she'd been in need. That thought alone should have been impetus enough to make her open her eyes and walk out the door.

Instead it made her pull him closer. Her heart knew what her mind had been hiding from all these years. Paul Sterling was the man to bring her from her sleep.

Those brief touches incited a firestorm in Angelica and she sought his mouth. He nibbled on her bottom lip, sucking gently on her flesh and sending shivers of awareness pulsing through her. Her breasts felt heavy and her scalp tight.

Paul's kiss consumed her like a wave on the sand. His arms held her like a current, soothing her and moving her gently against him. The warm pressure of his chest against her aching nipples was enough to make her melt.

"Mr. Sterling, your next appointment is here?"

The voice startled Angelica into standing. Paul walked back around his desk and hit a button on his phone. "Ask him to have a seat. I'm finishing up in here."

Angelica felt unkempt and tried to pat her hair back into its neat chignon. Her notebook lay on the floor and her bag had fallen to its side. Thankfully, none of the contents had spilled. Everything looked normal, but the world wasn't the familiar place it had been a mere five minutes earlier.

"Well..." he said.

Obviously he didn't know what to do with the situation either. Get it back to business, she thought. But how? Her pulse still raced, her body was still tingling and her mind was chaotic.

"Yes, well. I guess I have all the details to get to work on your party," she said, stooping to pick up her bag.

"Angel, I—"

"You have someone waiting and I really need to be going." She walked to the door and didn't look back. Couldn't look back because of what she might see on his face. She'd always prided herself on her self-control and now she knew that confidence was false. She'd been in control before because she hadn't been tempted.

The first time temptation visited her, she'd leaped for it with both hands, heedless of how hard she might fall.

"This isn't finished, Angelica," he said as she opened the door.

Glancing over her shoulder, she said, "I know."

Paul watched her go, realizing he'd made some major errors in judgment this morning. Not the least of which was following his gut instead of his brain. He never should have kissed her. And having kissed her he shouldn't have let her go before he'd drunk his fill. He would never be that foolish again.

Her eyes had been so sad, he knew he couldn't just let her leave. The last time he'd been responsible for putting that look in a woman's eyes had been the night of his sixteenth birthday when he'd taken his sister's car for a joyride and ended up in the county jail.

"Angelica, wait a moment."

But she'd already reached the elevator and looked as if she'd rather wait for Satan himself than Paul Sterling. His office was full of people and the last thing he should be doing was wasting time.

"Want me to go get her, Paul?" asked Corrine.

"No. I'll be right back." Dean Jenner, one of the directors who reported to him, was patiently waiting. "Dean, I'll be right back."

"No problem, boss."

Paul caught Angelica at the elevator. Her eyes were wild with embarrassment, passion and he thought a bit of anger. His stomach sank. He knew he was not hero material and the look in her eyes confirmed that she now shared his belief.

"I didn't mean for that to happen," he said. He really hadn't. She'd needed a shoulder to cry on and he'd offered one. But he hadn't counted on his reaction to her. Thought he'd be able to control his hormones in the office even though he hadn't had much luck with them on the dance floor. He should have known better.

There was something about Angelica Leone that

went straight through his system like ninety-proof whiskey.

"I know."

"I'm not usually so…well, let's just say I'm usually all business at work." There was no way he could say what was on his mind. There was something almost innocent about Angelica that he'd never encountered before. Though she was a woman, he didn't know what to say to her.

Since when couldn't he talk to a woman? And dammit, that's all she was to him. A woman, like any other. She was nothing special.

Even if her perfume did linger in the air after she left. Even if he did recall the feel of her in his arms even though he hadn't seen her in two days. Even though he'd just put her in front of his career and he'd never done that before.

"It's okay, really. Please don't make me talk about it right now."

"It doesn't feel okay, Angel."

"I wish you wouldn't call me that."

"Why not?"

"I'm nobody's angel."

"It feels like you could be mine."

The words startled him but he knew they were the truth. That scared him. Made him want to call back the words or make them seem less important. But there was no way he could. He had to live with them and hope she didn't realize what he'd meant.

"Every time I'm convinced you're the bad guy you put on that white hat of yours again."

"It's a costume," he said, needing to be honest with her because there was hope in her eyes. A hope that he knew would be wasted on him.

"Well, I'll make you a deal, I'll be your angel if you'll be my hero."

He swallowed against the need to kiss her again. He wanted to be her hero but knew he couldn't be. He couldn't tell her the reasons why, but he knew all the same that she'd be building false hope if she believed in him.

"I can't be that."

"I know you can be. It's just that you won't."

"Can't or won't, what's the difference?" he said, though he knew.

"'Won't' implies you're not interested in trying."

"Maybe I am but know I'll fail, and I never fail."

"Maybe this time you won't."

"I wouldn't hold my breath."

"Oh, Paul."

She touched his cheek. A tiny caress with her forefinger that spread quickly throughout his body. He was still semi-aroused from the kiss in his office. He wondered if he could kiss her again in the elevator. The bell rang and she stepped back.

The elevator was crowded when the doors opened. She tucked her bag under her arm and stepped into the car. "I'll call you with the details. Thanks for making time for me today."

She talked until the doors closed and Paul stood there in the hallway alone. The offices were quiet, as most people had gone to lunch. And though normally he appreciated the fact that he got an insane amount of work done while everyone else was gone, today he felt lonely.

He knew he had an appointment waiting back in his office and voice mails and e-mails to return, but that didn't stop the loneliness from surrounding him and reminding him that even if he made a place for Angelica in his life, it would only be temporary.

Four

Angelica had the feeling of narrowly escaping danger as she exited the crowded elevator. The lobby of Tarron was filled with employees and clients on their way to lunch. And she knew no one noticed her.

But her hands trembled and she had to stop by a potted plant and catch her breath before moving on. She hurried across the street to the parking garage and climbed into her '72 VW Bug.

The car didn't go with the image she liked to project for Corporate Spouses but there had to be something in her life that was just for her. Even if it was only her car. She had a vase that she filled every day with a fresh bud from her gardenia or rose bushes.

The scent filled her car. It reminded her of the lack of feminine scents in Paul's office. His space had been corporate and successful, not unlike a lot of other offices where she'd had meetings with executives since she'd founded her company. His space was so austere. Why?

There were no personal effects. Nothing that showed another side to Paul Sterling. It bothered her. The lack of something for her to pin her expectations on.

If he hadn't mentioned his boat, she'd have thought he never relaxed. *Oh, God…a yacht.* He wanted her to plan a party on his yacht. Though she lived in Florida she'd managed to successfully avoid spending any time near the water since Roger's death.

Not any longer.

She took a deep breath and started her car, easing out into the afternoon traffic. Her office was on Colonial Drive near the mall. She used rooms at Burdines for staging dinners and fashion consultations, so having her offices close to the mall made sense.

Her cell phone rang and she switched lanes before answering. The number wasn't one she recognized. "Hello?"

"It's Paul."

His voice tickled her ear and reminded her that less than fifteen minutes ago he'd kissed her. True, it had been a mistake, but a part of her didn't regret it. Although he was a client, he'd made her remember she was a woman, not only a *businesswoman*, the very thing she'd taken pains to forget.

"Did you remember a detail for your staff party?" she asked. *Please let that be why he's calling.*

"No."

She thought about pretending there was static on the line the way she did sometimes when her mother called to needle her about being single. But she wanted to hear what Paul had to say. She wanted another chance to prove to him that she was more than a businesswoman. She wanted to say something terribly brilliant and instead said, "Oh."

Silence buzzed on the open line. She heard the rustle of papers and then the click of keys on a keyboard. Was he checking his e-mail? He'd probably decided she'd donated her brain to science and couldn't be an asset to him in a social situation.

Why did he make her react as if he were her first big client?

"Paul, what did you want?" she asked, gathering her wits. She couldn't drive and talk at the same time, not to Paul, so she pulled into the parking lot of a fast-food restaurant and waited for his response.

"I wanted to apologize for my behavior again."

"Fine. I accept your apology. Let's not mention this again." Great, the one man to make her remember she's a woman regretted the kiss that had changed her. She didn't blame him. His office, his life had shown her what his words had implied, Paul Sterling lived a solitary life and liked it that way.

"Angelica…"

She didn't say anything because she didn't trust herself. The best plan, she thought, would be to pretend that they hadn't kissed. From now on she was going to be one hundred and ten percent professional.

"I've got to go. I'm at my office now and I have an appointment. I'll be in touch about the staff party once I have some details hammered out." She made a big deal out of turning off her car and jiggling the keys.

"Angelica, wait."

She didn't disconnect even though her instincts screamed for her to do so.

"Don't hang up angry."

"I'm not angry."

"So we're okay?"

"Sure. I think we'll work well together, and of course, keep our lips well away from each other's. That's the kind of behavior we frown on at Corporate Spouses."

"Not good for the image?" he asked dryly.

"Exactly. Once word gets around that you kiss one client you have to kiss them all," she said with a lightness she didn't come close to feeling.

"I'd never mention it," he said. The words sounded like a vow.

"I wish you could see yourself from my perspective," she said without thinking.

"What would I see?"

"A very caring man."

"Don't kid yourself, Angel. I care for no one."

"Everyone cares for someone."

"I don't. I stopped caring a long time ago. I like it that way."

If only she were still in his office. She wanted to see his eyes. To see the truth of what he was saying on his face. He couldn't really not care about people. He didn't strike her as a misanthrope, but that didn't mean he wasn't one.

"What about love?" she asked. Damn, she needed food or something to make her stop asking him questions.

"What about it?"

"Surely you're not ruling out love with caring, are you?"

"Love is a dangerous thing, Angel. No one knows that better than I and, yes, I am ruling it out."

"So that means you'll never marry?"

"Marriage and love are a recipe for disaster. But marriage by itself is part of my future."

"Really?"

"Sure, after I become CEO it'll be time to find a wife who looks at life the way I do."

"How's that, Paul?"

"The same way as running a company."

"That's no way to be happy."

"Who needs happy?"

"You do," she said softly. "Goodbye."

She disconnected the phone. Her emotions rocketing through her, telling her that she already cared too much for the man who disdained caring more than anything except love.

Lunch had not been the smartest idea, Paul admitted a week after the meeting in his office. Yet here he was sitting in the middle of the lunch-rush crowd with Angelica Leone. When she'd called to say she'd found a couple of gifts for the staff and wanted his opinion before ordering them, he'd been unable to resist seeing her again.

Images of her dark curly hair and brown eyes had dogged his sleep. On Friday he'd been in a meeting with a woman who'd been wearing the same perfume that Angelica had worn and again he'd found himself distracted from business by a woman—Angelica.

Never before had a woman gotten under his skin in such a way. In fact, no one woman had stood out among the crowd until now. It might be that her passionate lecture on caring had reminded him of his sister Layne's long-ago advice. Or maybe he was just tired from working too hard though usually he thrived on pressure.

Whatever the reason, here he was at Dexter's, a crowded lunch restaurant downtown, with Angelica sitting across from him. Even though the table was small, it allowed enough room so that their legs didn't bump under the tabletop. Paul stretched his legs on either side of hers feeling the slender length of her limbs against his own.

The eatery wasn't the least bit romantic and

teemed with corporate types, so it was about as safe as it could get. Why then was he becoming aroused from her proximity?

"I've never been here before," she said once they'd been seated.

"It's a good place for lunch. The atmosphere makes it great for relaxing clients."

"I hadn't thought of that."

"Well, with me it's all about business."

"I've noticed. How would you feel about doing me a favor?"

"Depends on the favor."

"We have monthly workshops at Corporate Spouses that feature different executives talking about their road to success. I'd love to have you be a part of our series."

"I'll think about it. I'm busy at the office right now."

"Well, we're scheduling into July right now. So it wouldn't be tomorrow night."

He nodded and took a sip of his iced tea. He'd rather have a beer, but he'd learned long ago that business meetings weren't the place for relaxing. Though his partnership with Angelica wasn't going to make or break him at Tarron, he knew he'd better be on the alert with her.

"Show me what you've come up with for the gifts."

"I've brought two samples today with different scripting on them."

He watched her mouth when she talked. Her lips

were painted a muted shade of red that was respectable. Except when brushed on her full lips—it was more tempting than the apple had been to Adam. *Damn*.

"Most of my staff has business-card cases," he said, gesturing to the first item she'd pulled from her large attaché.

"Don't discard this gift so quickly. There's something about pulling a business card from a monogrammed case that adds to your power in a meeting."

"I'll think about it. What else have you got?"

"These holders for PDAs. They'll fit all Palms and the knockoffs. I thought we could do a brass plate with an initial or first-name monogram on the front."

"Nice thinking. I gave my staff Palms for the holidays, so this would be perfect."

"Do you want leather or imitation?"

"What do you think?" he asked. He should just answer straight out, but he was still unsettled from that damn telephone conversation they'd had. The one where he'd come away feeling as if she knew him better than he'd ever wanted anyone to know him.

She eyed him up and down. His blood ran a little heavier as he withstood the female scrutiny in her gaze. She bit her bottom lip, that lush red piece of flesh he was dying to taste again. She couldn't possibly taste as incredible as his memories said she did.

"Leather," she said at last.

"Leather?" he asked, barely able to remember his name much less what they were talking about.

"Yes, leather. You'd want the real thing, first class all the way. Just like a Rolex or a European driving machine."

He shook his head to clear it. "You're right. Image is everything."

"I make my living thanks to that," she said with a smile.

He arched one eyebrow in question.

"If it weren't for image, I wouldn't have to train so many businessmen and women. I mean, if everyone were judged on skill alone then I'd have no one to train."

"Why don't you sound happy about that?"

"It makes me sad to think we live in a society that can be so shallow."

"Would you have us live the other extreme?"

"No, I guess not."

"The corporate world doesn't demand superficiality, only a certain sophistication. Would you trust your money to an unkempt man?"

"No," she said. She gathered up the items on the table.

"I'll need a list of names for the engraver," she said after she'd stowed her bag at her feet.

The bag brushed his leg and he shifted to make more room for her—his leg rubbing hers. The contact through layers of cloth was more frustrating than it should have been.

"I'll have Corrine send it to you by e-mail," he said, bringing his self-control back into play.

"Okay. I'll work with her to make sure there are no mistakes in the spelling of the names."

Their food arrived and the waitress left the check with their plates and then brought refills on the iced tea. Though it was almost March and probably cold elsewhere in the country, in Florida it was sunny and nice.

"I noticed your bag is leather."

"Well I like first class too," she said.

Her words cemented a thought he hadn't given much credence to. Possibly the solution was to make Angelica his in a very basic way. Then he could reclaim his perspective. "That's two things we have in common."

"What's the first?" she asked, taking a sip of her drink.

"Unless I'm mistaken, *passion.*"

She blinked at him and choked on her drink. Paul stood to pat her on the back and she looked up at him with questions in her eyes. He knew he needed more finesse than he'd ever used with any woman before. But he needed something from Angelica Leone that he'd never needed before.

Passion. The word echoed in her head like a mantra. Passion was the one thing she'd always hidden from. And now this man—Paul Sterling—tossed it around so carelessly. Mr.-I-don't-care-for-anyone.

Yet that very same attitude made her want to pour

her emotions over him. To saturate him with caring and affection until he realized that he couldn't live without it.

"I'm not sure what you want from me," she said after a moment had passed.

He leaned closer to her. The spicy scent of him, warm and masculine, assailed her. His legs once again enveloped hers under the table.

"I want the same chance you'd give any other man."

Her hands trembled, so she laced them together in her lap. She'd been feeling so confident of herself and her role in Paul's life. But you couldn't kiss a man and then walk away. She knew that.

"You're not another man," she said at last.

"Good of you to notice."

Their eyes met and she knew that he was asking her for something no other man ever had. She'd married Roger when she was a girl, barely twenty-one, and now at twenty-eight she had developed into a woman. But she'd had precious little experience with men. And here was one making her very aware of him and his masculinity.

"So what's the answer?" he asked.

"Was there a question? Because all I can remember is our conversation nearly a week ago when you told me that emotions have no part in your life." She took a sip of her iced tea and let the cool drink soothe her throat.

"Passion isn't really an emotion," he said. The seriousness in his posture and the intensity of his tone were at odds. And she realized that Paul Sterling was really two men warring under the very civilized skin that he showed the world.

One of those men was determined not to care for anyone—to be all business. The other was someone who couldn't help rescuing damsels and being gallant. Who would win the battle?

"I don't think I want to know what you classify it as…instinct, urge?" she asked.

His forehead wrinkled and he rubbed it. "This isn't going at all as I'd planned."

"How did you ever think it could? You can't predict how I'll react to a situation. We don't know each other."

He sighed. The sound made her want to agree to whatever he asked of her. The sound made her want to tame the savage beast that she sensed waited just under the surface inside him. She wanted—heck, she wanted him and he was off limits.

"I'm asking you to give me a chance."

She took a deep breath, unlaced her fingers and placed them firmly on the table. She wasn't normally so easily shaken, but from the first, Paul had touched parts of her that were vulnerable. Honesty was the best policy, she thought. Paul's natural heroic streak would take over.

"You make me feel things I'd forgotten about. But for me that kind of passion comes with a high risk. I'd chance it for the right man. Unfortunately you're not him."

"Who is?" he asked.

Dealing with men was harder than she remembered. She had to walk a careful line here and not just for the sake of her business.

"I haven't met him yet. I just know the next time I get involved passionately with a man it'll be because of more than lust."

He placed one of his large hands over hers. Caressing her knuckles with his forefinger. Shivers ran up her arm and her nipple tightened against her bra. Her first instinct was to jerk her hand away. She acknowledged that she was a little shocked by the intimate reactions she felt. It had been more than seven years since she'd felt anything that intense.

"I feel more than lust for you."

"Prove it."

"How am I supposed to do that?"

"I don't know. I just know that you're the one who warned me off. Why the change of heart?"

"You're interfering with my job."

"What did you say?"

"I can't concentrate at work because you've been on my mind."

She was flattered on a certain level and insulted at the same time. "Paul, you need to enroll in a class on people skills."

"Not winning friends and influencing people at this table?"

"Certainly not."

"Will you at least think about what I've said?"

"I doubt I could ignore your words even if I

wanted to. For the record, exactly what are you asking me for? A one-night stand? A red-hot affair?"

"A committed long-term arrangement until one or both of us wants out."

"Given this some thought, huh?"

"I mentioned that I haven't been able to focus on work. That's intolerable. This is the only solution I can think of."

"Well, I need more than that from a man."

"I'm willing to negotiate."

"You have a reputation of being a shark."

He shrugged. "I'm harmless where you're concerned."

"My fear is that you aren't."

"Think about it, Angel. You can give me your answer in two weeks at our first official outing for Corporate Spouses."

She nodded and luckily Paul's cell phone rang. She tugged her hand from under his, tossed a few bills on the table, stood up and walked away. She hoped he didn't realize that she was running away from him, but knew he was smart enough to recognize a retreat when he saw one.

Five

Angelica had managed to neatly avoid being alone with Paul since his unexpected and totally arousing proposal at their lunch. But that didn't change the fact that they had to work together. Or the fact that she wanted something more from him.

He'd sent her flowers— a bouquet of spring blooms. Which had pretty much crumbled her defenses. There hadn't been any fancy words on the card, just simple ones... *Think about my offer.*

She wasn't sorry he'd made the offer, only that it had come out of the blue and at a time when she couldn't take him up on it. She didn't know that there ever would have been a right time and that made her a little sad because there was something about Paul Sterling that she wanted to get to know much better.

Today she'd have to deal with him face-to-face and not in her dreams. Today she'd have to tackle her biggest fear, being near water, and what was growing into her second biggest—Paul Sterling. Today as he moved through the crowd of his staff and their significant others, she realized that she wanted to accept his offer of a red-hot affair.

She had accepted his wish to hold the party at the yacht club instead of on his yacht. The club was on one of the larger lakes on the Butler chain. It was set on an inlet with water on three sides. Huge glass windows afforded the people inside an undisturbed view of the lake. Angelica had managed to spend the last hour in the kitchen supervising a staff that needed no direction from her.

For the first time since she'd opened Corporate Spouses she felt incapable of doing her job. That irritated her enough to send her through the swinging doors into the crowded reception room. She took a deep breath and walked along the buffet table making sure the food was set out properly. Then double-checked the gift bags that bore the name of each member of Paul's staff. Rand was passing out the gifts and double-checking the names.

Paul stood across the room talking to a very distinguished-looking gentleman. She thought it was Tom Tarron, founder and CEO of Tarron Enterprises, but she couldn't be sure from this distance. She glanced away from Paul and caught the sun's reflection off the softly lapping waves of the lake.

Cold chills slithered down her spine. Her feet suddenly felt like lead weights and she knew that she couldn't move. She felt the ripples of the water around her, felt herself being tugged deeper and deeper in the water's cool grasp.

"Angel?" Paul asked.

How he'd gotten across the room, she didn't know. She only knew that his eyes compelled her to look at him. She did. She watched him and felt the fear that had threatened her ebb.

"Damn. You're making me feel like the Marquis de Sade."

"Not your fault," she said through clenched teeth.

He cupped her jaw, tilting her face up toward his. His eyes caressed her and she tried to forget about the water. Tried to forget that the last time she'd been in Paul's presence he'd asked her to share the most intimate part of herself with him. Tried to forget that it had been years since any man had wanted her for more than a "corporate wife."

But if she accepted Paul's offer wasn't that all she'd be? Once again she'd settle for the facade of a real relationship and the safety of a business one.

"I should have listened when you said you couldn't go near water," he said.

She shook her head. "Seven years is too long."

"You're right. I just wish I wasn't the one forcing you to face your devil."

Honesty compelled her to admit, "I can't think of anyone else I'd rather have at my side."

He looked at her askance and she knew she'd said too much. It was too late, however, to call back the words.

"We'll talk after the party," he said.

She was helpless to do more than nod.

"Keep your eyes on me," he said, leading her across the room. Soon she was positioned with her back to the windows and the party had the look of many she'd hosted in the past.

"Thank you."

"You're welcome."

Paul introduced her to two of his staffers and then went to mingle. Angelica felt fine knowing that she was on familiar turf. It was easy to see that Paul's group loved what they did. They talked easily amongst themselves, laughed easily and treated Paul with the kind of respect that leaders didn't command but earned.

Angelica moved around the room, careful to keep her back to the windows, when she noticed a man in the corner. Paul caught her eye and she nodded to let him know she'd take care of the man. It was funny how they communicated effortlessly as if they'd been doing this sort of thing for years.

As if they'd known each other forever and maybe lifetimes before, she thought. Then dismissed the thought. Paul Sterling wasn't her soul mate. He wasn't yang to her yin. She'd had that once and soul mates didn't come along more than once in a lifetime.

Angelica chatted up the man in the corner, learning that he was Paul's business manager, Fred Smith. Fred was more comfortable with figures than people. She smiled at him, leading him from the corner to a data programmer Angelica had met earlier. The woman, Tammy Conner, was also shy and not comfortable in a social setting. After Angelica had them together, she brought the conversation around to a new program that Tammy was working on to make the rolling five-year plan easier to manipulate.

The two of them were soon engrossed in a topic that Angelica really didn't understand. She smiled and started to move away.

"Nice work," Paul said, handing her a glass of Pinot Grigio.

"Thanks. I love matching people up."

"At functions?"

"And in life. Not many people share your perspective on life and marriage. Most are looking for someone to share their life."

"I am too."

"Not with emotions."

He arched one eyebrow at her. "We'll never see eye-to-eye on this topic."

"What would it take to convince you?"

"I don't know," he said. The honesty in his eyes convinced her that if she decided to take on Paul Sterling, it would take all she had to break through the barrier he had around himself. And there was no guarantee that she'd succeed.

* * *

Tom Tarron was one of the biggest influences in Paul's professional life. He'd started working for Tom on an internship in college and had found someone to emulate. He was honest enough to admit that having Tom take him under his wing that first summer had a made a difference in his life. Tom was smooth, dressing for success from the top of his sandy blond hair to his hand-sewn Italian shoes. Paul's mother had been in the final stages of cervical cancer. Between school and his mother's illness, work had become a refuge.

But Tom had one thing that Paul would never have. A deep and abiding love for his wife, Chancey. Paul never understood how a man so savvy in the business world would allow himself to be so weak on a personal front. Yet he knew that Chancey was the reason Tom had worked so hard.

Tom had confided once his belief that all men aren't whole until they have a woman to share their lives. The two men had decided to disagree on the subject and Paul had avoided personal-life discussions with Tom after that.

"Great party, Paul." Tom said. "I really like your date. She's just the kind of woman who'd make the perfect wife for an executive."

Paul looked out at the lake. The afternoon sun reflected through the windows. "In a manner of speaking she already is."

"I know about her business. It would make her a valuable asset to you as your career grows."

"Tom, I have it on feminine authority that women don't like to be referred to as assets."

"Not to their faces," Tom added.

"I guess a smart man would know that."

"There's smart and there's smart. Women have a way of making you forget things," Tom said. The older man surveyed the room.

"Tell me about it," Paul said.

"Is she the one for you?" Tom asked, his gray-green eyes putting Paul on the spot. Suddenly Paul felt like a very junior executive making his first big presentation.

Paul shook his head. "I don't believe that woman exists."

"Sure she does. But you have to want to find her, Paul."

Paul downed his scotch in one gulp. He longed for the bottle so he could drink more, although he knew firsthand alcohol wasn't an answer. Instead he rubbed his eyebrows and watched the woman who'd sparked this discussion. She moved with the kind of feminine grace that had intrigued men for centuries.

There was an aura of mystery that surrounded her. He wanted to dive deeper and unravel her secrets one by one. To find what made her tick so that he could understand her completely and then maybe he'd feel safe with her.

"It looks like Chancey needs rescuing," Tom said. "Think about what I said."

Paul watched Tom leave knowing his boss and friend was only trying to help, but he didn't need advice on his life. He knew what worked and why. He didn't want a woman in his life who would demand more from him than nights of hot sex and money. Something told him Angelica would want more. She had pretty much said it in no uncertain terms.

Paul made a circuit around the room, hearing nothing but good comments about Angelica. Everyone seemed to be enjoying themselves. Paul felt a wave of satisfaction sweep through him. His anniversary with Tarron was how he marked time. Everything that had happened prior to his joining the company was a dark wasteland he preferred not to visit. His days at Tarron were the stuff dreams were made of and this celebration was the icing on the cake.

"What do you think?" Angelica asked.

"Pretty good work for someone who spent the first part of the event in the kitchen."

"Worried you hadn't gotten your money's worth?" she teased.

"For an instant. But I've seen you in action before."

"When?"

He almost smiled. "The night of the auction. Anyone who can fall off the stage and then get up and pitch her business is someone who can conquer any fear."

"I wish I had your faith," she said. He knew that she did have faith. Only someone with immense self-confidence could start their own business and make it a success.

"You don't need it."

"Yes I do. I haven't been able to look out the windows."

"Everyone has a weakness."

"Even you?"

He shrugged, he wasn't about to tell her what his weaknesses were. He was already too susceptible to her. "If you want, after the party's over I'll help you."

"Not going to tell me what your weakness is?"

"Angel, we were talking about you."

"We were talking about us."

"I must have missed that."

"Aren't you the man who asked me to give having an affair with him a try?"

His body tightened at her words. Though he'd said little else to her about the subject, all of his thoughts dwelled on it. Of course, he'd been turned down before by women he'd wanted, but right now it seemed he'd never wanted any woman as much as he wanted Angelica. "I am."

"Sharing is a good way to encourage me," she said.

"I don't like to be vulnerable."

"No one does. But it builds trust."

"How will knowing my weakness help you to trust me. I'd rather help you over your fear."

"I know," she said.

He had the feeling he'd just failed a test. "I told you I wasn't your hero."

"You could be," she said, then turned to walk away.

Her words echoed in his mind. He had the feeling he'd just met his biggest weakness and she had no idea.

Angelica waved goodbye to the caterer and started toward her car. Despite what Paul had said about hanging around afterward, she hadn't seen him since his last guest had left. And maybe that was for the best.

Hell, she knew it was for the best. But just once she'd wanted to have a man follow through. A part of her, no matter how irrational it sounded, had always resented Roger for promising to spend his life with her and then leaving. She knew he'd had no choice in death but she couldn't get over that tiny resentment in her heart.

She opened the door of her VW. Waves of heat came out of the car. March—and already Florida was hot. She rolled down the windows and leaned on the front of her car. The lake was out there. She couldn't see it from her vantage point but she knew it was just on the other side of the building.

She heard the sound of a motorboat and it brought back memories. Today she pushed them aside. Obviously this wasn't going to be a fear she could battle past easily. Then again, most things worth having weren't easily won.

"Is this a private party or can anyone crash?" Paul asked.

"Sorry, invitation only."

He smiled, slipped his hand into his pocket and pulled an imaginary envelope from his pocket. "I don't have an invite but I do have this coupon."

She reached out and pretended to take the coupon from him. She didn't meet his eyes, afraid she would see something there that she couldn't deal with right now.

"I can't read the writing," she said.

"You've got it upside down," he said, taking the imaginary coupon back and studying it.

"It says that it's good for the banishment of one fear."

"Does it expire?" she asked. She wanted to conquer her fear and she wanted to do it with Paul by her side.

"Afraid so. Good today only."

"That's just the way wishes are, never exactly what you asked for or how you expect them to come."

"I know I'm not much of a genie but surely you'll agree I do have my moments."

"You have many of them, Paul. But I thought you didn't want to discuss that."

"I'm new to this business of granting wishes. It seems to me that you…shouldn't look a gift horse in the mouth."

"Point taken."

He held out his hand. She couldn't see his eyes

behind his dark sunglass lenses and a part of her was very glad, though another part longed to see what he was thinking. She reached out for his hand. And then realized what she was about to do.

"I don't know if I can do it."

"I won't let go of you."

"Promise?" She sounded small to her own ears and she disliked the feeling immensely, but as soon as her fingers touched Paul's his warmth spread throughout her.

"Promise," he said, brushing his lips against the back of her hand.

"Tell me what you fear most."

"The sounds."

"Which ones?"

"The engine of the speedboat, the lapping of the waves. Skis sliding up the ramp."

He kept them moving slowly toward the lake. When they reached the corner of the yacht club, she froze. Move, feet, she commanded, but they wouldn't. Jerking her hand from his grasp, she leaned back against the hot wall of the building and buried her head in her hands.

"I can't do this."

Paul sighed. She felt his body brush hers as he leaned against the wall beside her. "You have to think about something else."

"What? Roger and I were childhood sweethearts. We grew up swimming, skiing and snorkeling together. Every memory I have of water is associated with him in some way."

"You must have one memory without him."

"No. Not one." She felt her breaths coming in short and shallow. She had to calm down. But she couldn't stop the memories. It was as if she'd evoked that horrible day and now they flooded her. The boat, the jump, the horrible crash and then the last sight of Roger as he slid beneath the water's surface. Of course she'd seen him again in the funeral home but that hadn't really been Roger.

Paul gripped her face, forced her to look at him. He'd removed his shades and he pushed her glasses up on her head so that their eyes could meet without barriers. "Look at me."

Helpless to do other than he commanded, she watched his gaze narrow on her. "The first time I entered the water I was seven years old. I couldn't swim and I was scared of sharks because I'd seen *Jaws* two nights earlier. My old man was with me.

"He hung on to my hand as the waves rushed past our legs. He couldn't swim either but he didn't let fear stop him. He just held me and we stood there until I realized there was nothing scary about the water. The next week we started swim lessons."

Angelica saw in her mind's eye a little boy with Paul's dark hair and tough expression, clinging to his father's hand. She had stood on sandy beaches herself, always with Roger. Now in her mind she saw herself holding hands with Paul. Not the child Paul in her image but the man here with her now.

"I don't know the way around this fear, but like

my old man, I'll hold on to you until you've faced it.''

She nodded. "I'm ready to try again."

They walked slowly toward the lakeshore. Angelica focused on the man holding her hand in real time and in her dreamscape. The man who was standing next to the water's edge. The man whose hand was solid and steady in a way that he'd warned her he could never be in life.

Six

Paul was flying blind and he didn't like it. Angelica's hand in his grasp felt small and distinctly feminine, calling to the fore everything masculine in him. He'd never been in a situation like this and if he worked things right he never would be again.

He tried to slide his hand from her grasp but she held tightly to his fingers. He sensed she was drawing strength from him. He didn't begrudge her whatever she needed to deal with her fear. And although he knew it wasn't chivalrous, he wanted to help her forget the past with passion. He wanted to taste her sweet lips. To once again delve into the depths of her mouth and taste her.

He wanted more than that but a kiss would be a nice place to start.

She stared at the water lapping against the dock as if it held secrets that she needed to unlock. Yet he knew she was aware of him. He didn't want to break the silence that had settled around them. His first impulse was to pull her into his arms and let nature take its course but he didn't act on it.

He didn't know what she was thinking and maybe that was why it was so hard to trust anyone, especially a woman. With men at least he knew how they thought, the processes they used to draw conclusions, make plans and take action. Women had always been a mystery to him.

He'd grown up in a house filled with women. His mother and sister were big influences on his life. He didn't tell Angelica, but his father had been killed three weeks after the swim lessons he'd told her about. His father's death had drastically changed life in the Sterling household.

Angelica shivered and his father's advice came back to him. *It's our job to take care of the women.* I'm trying, Dad. I'm trying.

He shrugged out of his sport jacket and draped it over Angelica's shoulders. There was something about her that brought out forgotten gestures. Gallant gestures that he remembered between his father and mother.

"Thanks," she said.

He wanted to leave here—as fast as he could. Just escape from Angelica and the bonds she wove between them. He also wanted to be able to look into her eyes and see peace not troubled waters.

"Want to sit down?" he asked.

She lowered herself to the dock and he sat next to her. The lake water was lower than it would be in summer, though not dangerously low. The sun was sinking low on the horizon and the sounds of whippoorwills and crickets began to fill the night air. She reached out and clasped his hand to hers again.

"Did you know that in medieval times water was an analogy for love?" she said.

"No. I was never too keen on the past. I prefer to look to the future."

"Well, it was. I read everything I could the year after Roger died, trying to make sense of his death."

"Are you trying to tell me something?"

"No. I was just thinking that you don't fear the water…"

"So it follows I don't fear love?"

"It sounds hokey when you say it out loud."

He nodded. "Don't put too much stock in my love of water, Angel."

"Why not?"

"I grew up in Florida. I've always been around the water."

"Me too," she said.

"Not many of us natives around," he said, grateful she gave him an avenue to change the topic.

"Must be why we bonded," she said.

Damn, she'd led him back to the one place he didn't want to be. "You think so?"

She bit her lip as if she wanted to say more but didn't. He realized he wanted her to keep talking.

Maybe she'd say something that would make it easier for him to understand what was going on in her head.

He worried for a minute that fear was overtaking her again. That she was drifting into the past where he couldn't reach her. Into the past that was dominated by a man who understood love and affection and wasn't afraid to give her what she needed. A man that Paul knew he could never compete with.

"Want to talk about the water again?" he asked carefully.

"Do you?"

"Not if you're going to draw more love analogies. The truth is I don't want to see fear on your face again."

"Okay. No love and no fear. That should be easy enough."

He had a feeling it wasn't going to be easy. "Why is it that the things we expect to be easy never are?"

"Because we don't respect them," she said.

"You might be right," he said. He had nothing but respect for this woman who had worked hard to get over a fear. To take back her life. Had he ever tried to take back his life? He knew that he'd never say it out loud but his greatest fear wasn't commitment, it was being left alone the way his mother had been when his father died.

Silence grew between them again and after a time she withdrew her hand from his. Though that was the very thing he'd wanted earlier, he felt bereft from the loss. That angered him. He clenched his hands then pushed to his feet, shoving his hands deep into his pockets.

She wants different things from a relationship than you do, he reminded himself, but right now that didn't matter.

She stood as well. Pulled her sunglasses down over her eyes. "Thank you. This is different than I thought it would be."

"Good or bad?"

She didn't answer and that lack of response echoed in his mind. They walked carefully back to her car. "It wasn't bad."

She opened the door and he knew he should let her go. That to preserve the kind of life he liked living, he needed distance from her. He reached out anyway, stopping her with his hand on her elbow.

She turned and looked up at him. Slowly he lowered his head.

Angelica knew she was operating at gut level instead of with the common sense she'd relied on for her entire life. But she needed to feel Paul's mouth on hers. She needed to physically feel him against her.

He angled his head, tilting her head back, supporting her with his palm at her neck. She wasn't uncomfortable but she was completely under his power. He controlled the embrace, the depth of the kiss and her to some extent.

She shivered as his tongue brushed hers and he tasted her so deeply that she had a hard time figuring out where she ended and he began. She moaned deep in her throat and moved sensually against him.

He trembled under her touch. She slid her hands over his shoulders and down his back. Muscles tensed in his biceps where he held her and she marveled at his strength. So strong on the outside yet she knew he'd be tender in caring if only he'd allow himself.

The memories, the party, his sensual invitation were playing havoc with her normal equilibrium. And she found herself needing something solid to anchor her. Someone to hold on to. Someone to cling to. Not just anyone, she realized as his hands traveled down her back, but only one man—Paul Sterling.

He shifted so that he was leaning on the hood of her car and cradled her between his legs. She felt the hardness of his erection. It called an answering heat from her body. Control slipped away from her. Overwhelmed by Paul, she pulled back, breaking the kiss.

He stared down at her, their bodies still intimately pressed together. His eyes were hidden behind his sunglasses and she wished they weren't. She knew he rarely let any emotion show on his face and needed to believe that maybe this once she'd affected him so deeply that she could see a change.

''What was that for?'' she asked.

He didn't answer, just rubbed his thumb along her lower lip. Tingles spread down her neck and arms. Her nipples beaded under her lined jacket. She clenched her thighs and knew that unless something cataclysmic happened in the next few minutes she'd agree to whatever Paul wanted.

"To remind us both I'm not a good guy."

"I haven't forgotten," she said. Knowing that fate had once again stepped in.

She reminded herself she was a realist and that you couldn't force someone to change. In fact, she wasn't sure she even wanted to try. But today as he'd stood next to the lake letting her draw on his strength, Paul had touched something deep inside her and she wanted to give him back something.

Only he wanted lust from her.

"Why so sad, Angel?" he asked. His voice was deeper than usual and brushed over her aroused senses like a silk shirt on naked skin.

She stepped away from him. For a second she missed the heat of his body. But as she stood apart she began to feel normal again. Standing on her own was what she'd learned to do best.

She thought about hedging. Then decided that if Paul was worth her time, and her instincts said he was, then he deserved honesty from her. "I'm looking for a man who wants me enough to stick around."

"I offered to stay."

He had and she was grateful he'd been so honest with her, but she knew that she needed more than he could give. And it was time for her to make a decision. "For the short term. I need more than that."

"Hasn't your life proved that the short term is all anyone gets?" he asked.

His words cut to her heart. She knew he was right. She had told herself the same thing many times but she'd always held her breath, hoping for someone to prove her wrong. "Others have more than short term."

"Maybe we all only get a certain kind of luck. You know what they say, 'lucky in love, unlucky in business.'"

"I thought it was 'unlucky in cards,'" she said to avoid the truth in his words.

"Cards, business, what's the difference?"

"I've never thought of it that way. Do you think we only get to be lucky in one aspect of our life?"

"You are very good at business."

"You may be right. Maybe I should give up on love, like you have."

"Why would you do that?"

"I'm just tired of staring at the same facts and hoping for something that'll never come true."

"Hey, Angel, don't let my attitude bring you down."

"It's not just you. It's the lake and everything."

He rubbed his jaw and then glanced out at the lake. "Frederick Douglass said, 'If there is no struggle, there is no progress.'"

"What are you trying to tell me?" she asked.

"Nothing comes from nothing. You have to have love to give and receive it. You have that. I don't."

"Why not?"

"I cut myself off from it when my dad died."

"When was that?"

"When I was seven."

"How did you stop caring?"

"I didn't at first. I just watched loving a man who wasn't there anymore kill my mom slowly. I promised myself never to be that weak and I never have."

"Not everyone views love as a weakness."

"I know that's why you shouldn't give up on it. The right man is out there."

"And you're not the man for me, Paul Sterling?"

"I guess not."

"But there's a side of you that could be."

"I have potential?"

"Something like that. And I'm tempted to teach you to love again."

"Why only tempted?"

"I'm not sure you'd really try. I might put all that energy into a man who only took the one thing he wanted from me."

"Ah, the lust thing, right?"

"You did ask me to have an affair with you."

"And you're never going to forget it, are you?" he asked, but his tone was light, almost teasing.

"It was my first such offer," she said.

"I'm glad to be your first."

She opened her car door again and started to get inside. "What do you say I teach you all you've forgotten about love?"

"I'm not sure I want to remember. But I do want to get to know you better."

"Are you going to make me a deal, Sterling?"

"Oh, yes."

"I've been warned not to negotiate with a shark."

"Want to hear the details or not?"

"I'm listening."

"We get together away from this business arrangement. Whatever happens, happens."

"How does that help me?"

"You show me love and I'll show you reality."

"Thank you but I'm acquainted with reality."

"Not mine."

She thought about his proposal for a minute. She wanted Paul. Wanted his laughter, keen intelligence and kisses. She knew that even if she didn't agree to see him she'd be thinking about him. And the chance to unlock the well of caring she sensed deep inside Paul was too much to resist.

"You've got yourself a deal."

Angelica's words echoed in his mind. It was not like the closing of any other deal he'd ever negotiated. He had no idea how to proceed. Should he ask for terms? That might be taking matters too far.

In essence they'd changed nothing. There wasn't an open invitation to seduction. Yet, at the same time, he knew he'd tacitly agreed to let her try to make him care again. He only hoped he could hold up his end of the bargain. He'd always met contracted terms before. He vowed that she wasn't going to be the first person with whom he failed to meet an obligation.

He had the feeling that he'd disappoint her. Maybe she'd disappoint him and prove that he couldn't love. Deep down he sensed that if anyone could make him care it was Angelica Leone. Watching her at the party this afternoon had proven that she was the real thing.

She didn't mingle like a socialite. She'd genuinely listened to what people had to say. When she'd drawn Fred into the party, something that he'd never seen Fred do before, he'd been amazed.

Then he'd started really observing her. It wasn't business gimmicks she was using in there. Angelica was the real deal. She smiled at the guests and made them feel important not out of anything other than her own authentic interest in them.

What the hell had he been thinking? He closed her car door. She looked up at him, her head tilted at an angle that was perfect for a kiss. He wanted— no, needed to taste her again but didn't give in to the impulse. Too much had happened here this afternoon.

"I'll follow you home," he said, straightening before he did something he knew he shouldn't.

He could tell his words shocked her. Her skin flushed and her fingers drummed nervously on the edge of the door. He wished he'd meant them as she'd obviously taken his words. He'd love nothing more than to follow her to her home and make love with her. Except that everything about her inspired the protective side of him.

She was a woman to be cherished. Why then did

he want to ravish her? Why then could he think of nothing else but pushing past the barriers she had constructed and finding the elemental woman underneath? Why then did the thought of this woman leave him aching?

"I have an event tonight. I can't see you," she said as she tucked a strand of hair behind her ear. He watched the gesture. It was something he noticed she did when she was nervous.

He didn't want to unnerve her but at the same time relished the thought that he affected her. It was only fair, since she'd made him look harder at his own life than anyone else ever had. She'd even influenced Tom Tarron. Tom had been grooming Paul for the CEO position for the last year. Only today had Tom mentioned spouses.

The few times the subject had come up in the past it had sounded as if Tom could care less one way or another if his senior vice president was married. But today, Paul had felt Tom found him lacking. He knew Tom admired his ambition and he wasn't sure how to balance a life in which he didn't totally focus on work.

Angelica looked up at him expectantly.

"I meant I'd make sure you got home safely. I have to go in to the office and get some things done." He'd been at the office this morning before the party. But there was always work to be done. And he'd rather spend time there than in his condo alone.

"Oh. Well, I don't want to keep you from anything important."

"You won't," he said without thinking.

She recoiled. "Boy, you know how to make a girl feel special."

"I can always work," he said. He hadn't meant the words the way they sounded. But he needed to deal with her honestly. Nothing came between him and his career.

"And you always do, is that it?" she asked.

He shoved his hands into his pockets and glanced across the parking lot where his Mercedes was parked. The car was like everything else in his life. An expensive accessory he used to fill the empty spaces. But at Tarron he felt whole. He didn't need luxury items in his office. "My job is my life."

"I'll have to remember that. You don't do anything away from the office?"

"I have the yacht. It's a great stress reliever to be out on the water, away from the office and tension. Actually, I feel energized by the kind of stress that comes from running a multimillion dollar business."

"And no woman can compete with that," she said.

"I've never met one."

"What have I gotten myself into?"

"Feeling like you've made a deal with the devil?" he asked.

"You're no devil, Paul."

"Sometimes you make me feel that way. Maybe we should end this before it begins."

"You're the first man I've wanted to get to know better since Roger died. Something tells me you'll be worth it."

"I hope I can live up to that. But I'm only human."

"I didn't think you knew that."

"Of course I do. That's why I keep myself separate from others."

"I won't hurt you."

"You can't stop fate, Angel."

"I know," she said.

"Drive carefully. I'll be behind you the entire way."

He pivoted and walked away from her. He knew she watched him leave and he wondered what she saw in him that he missed in the mirror. Even though she hadn't said it out loud, his gut said she trusted him on a personal level. And he couldn't remember the last time that had happened.

Seven

Angelica waited for Paul to call her. Surely a man who'd bargained for a personal relationship would call. She'd expected him to pursue her now that she'd given him carte blanche but he hadn't been kidding when he'd said his job was his life. Even though he'd intimated that he wanted a personal relationship with her he'd made no steps toward that end.

By Thursday she realized that he'd have time for her when he wasn't busy. And that might be never. Her part of the bargain was to show him how to care and, hopefully, love, but first she had to show him how to live. She had no idea how to start.

She'd never been the aggressor in any relationship that wasn't business. She wondered if she could apply those skills to Paul. *Would he respond the same way Rand did when she wouldn't back down at work?*

"Kelly, can you get Rand for me?" she called to her secretary.

"Sure thing, boss lady." Kelly was cheeky and lacked respect for her elders. She was also fun to work with and gave the office an energy that only someone who was twenty-one and working in an office for the first time could.

"You rang?" Rand asked, appearing in the door. He was dressed in his usual uniform, Hugo Boss suit and Armani dress shirt. With his green eyes and dark as night hair, Rand could have been a movie star. Rand had grown up understanding that clothes made the man and it was very apparent in the way he dressed. His collar was open and in his left hand he held a rainbow of silk ties.

"Are you teaching knot tying again?" she asked, knowing it was Rand's least favorite class.

"I lost a bet."

"You lost a bet?"

"Believe it or not. Did you call me in here to gloat?"

"No. Are the Magic season tickets available for tonight's game against the Lakers?" she asked. Corporate Spouses held season tickets to all major-league sporting teams and for the opera and Broadway series. They often used the events as a final test for their clients.

"Sort of. No one is scheduled for a final tonight and I was planning to use them."

"Good, do you mind if I have them?"

"Yes. You don't have the proper respect for L.A."

"Rand, did you meet the two guys we're training to take your place...oops, I meant, to help you out."

"Of all the things I'm afraid of, Angelica, you firing me is not one of them. My brother drew up our partnership papers, remember?"

"This is for a good cause," she said. Who had she been kidding when she'd thought that Rand backed down for her at work? Men were one big mystery to her and she had no idea what made them tick.

"The Lakers are my team."

"Come on. I put up with you hanging a banner over the door last year when they won the playoffs, didn't I?"

"Why do you need the tickets?" he asked, propping one shoulder against the door.

"It's personal."

"Oh ho. *Personal.* Is it a man?"

"That's none of your business."

"Excuse me, but didn't I go on a blind date last weekend with Marjorie from your yoga class. Marjorie who you said, and I quote, 'is just perfect for you.'"

"You didn't like her?"

"She was okay. But if you can pry into my life..."

"Turnabout and all that?"

"Oh, yeah. So who's the guy?"

"Paul Sterling."

"You're kidding. What happened to *Don't let the client get personal?*"

She glared at Rand.

He shrugged at her then pulled the tickets from his pocket. "Have fun, kiddo."

"I'm not sure he'll go."

"He will."

"How do you know?"

"You wouldn't waste time asking a man who wasn't interested."

Rand left her office, closing the door behind him. Angelica looked at the tickets in her hand. Lower mezzanine. Even after Shaq had left Orlando they were still good seats.

She picked up the phone and dialed Paul's business number before she could change her mind. She'd never asked a man out before. Corrine answered and put her on hold. It seemed like thirty minutes had passed by, the clock on the wall had only clicked one minute when Paul picked up.

"Hello?"

"Paul, it's Angelica."

"What can I do for you?" he asked.

She couldn't think. Focus, she thought. Focus on business and then you can ease into the whole date thing. "I wanted to talk to you about the second contracted date we have."

"Yes. I've been thinking of using your domestic

cleaning service instead of a date. Would that be okay?''

That didn't fit with the Paul she was coming to know. "Sure. Why?''

"I'm going out of town for two weeks.''

Oh. Although she hadn't seen him in five days, still she'd liked knowing he was in the same city she was. "Where are you going?''

"London.''

"Very well. I'll arrange for your condo to be cleaned. Leave your keys with your secretary and I'll pick them up from her. When do you leave?''

"Sunday.''

"Are you busy tonight?'' she asked before she could chicken out.

"I was planning to work late.''

"Remember our bargain?'' she asked.

Silence buzzed on the line. "Yes.''

"Well, my part of the deal was to show you how to live. I've got two tickets to tonight's Magic game.''

"You're not taking no for an answer, is that it?''

"I don't want to muscle you into going out with me.''

He laughed. "I'm quivering from your intimidation tactics.''

"Okay, so I'm not scary. Will you go out with me tonight? No business—just basketball, beer and some lousy pizza.''

"Yes,'' he said.

* * *

Paul cursed time as he sped through the almost deserted streets of Orlando toward the T. D. Waterhouse Center. He parked his car and sprinted toward the building. Why was he in a hurry to meet her?

He knew why. When he'd left her on Saturday he'd had a hope that had been dead a long time. The hope that spring might now be a part of his life instead of the long winter that he'd existed in. Today when she'd called, he realized that she was still interested in him. That she'd made a choice. It was his turn to step up to the plate.

But old habits died hard and when Tom had called a last-minute dinner meeting, Paul couldn't say no. Angelica had left his ticket with Corrine and Corrine had given him a harsh look that said she didn't approve of his actions. He'd ignored her.

Corrine did like the promotions they both kept getting. And dinner meetings made the difference between promotion and stagnation. The client, Pete Macneilly, was one of the first Tarron had worked with. A huge metals manufacturer who had helped put Tarron on the map when Tom had first opened his doors in the late 1950s. Paul could have begged off, but Tom was grooming him to take over and Macneilly was more than a strategic account. It was a very important partnership.

Walking out early wasn't an option. According to the radio station he'd listened to, they were in the second half of the game. If he was lucky, he'd get to his seat before it ended.

Damn. Of all the nights for her to have called.

Maybe he should have made the opening gesture in this relationship they were developing, but with his trip to London his focus had to be on the office situation.

Angelica knew what his life was like. That didn't stop the guilt. His sister, Layne, hated it when her husband, a fisherman off the shores of Gloucester in Maine, was out late. The demands of the job didn't matter to her, she always wanted her man home with her at night. He couldn't imagine that Angelica would feel differently.

Though he wasn't yet her man. He wanted to be. And maybe that was why he was so concerned about being late. If any other woman waited for him at the game, he'd have canceled the date earlier tonight. He wouldn't have even tried to make everything happen in one night.

But it wasn't another woman. It was Angelica and she brought out parts of him that he didn't even realize he had. The meeting had run late. Later than he'd expected. He'd made no bones about the fact that his career came first.

Did he sound defensive?

He left his jacket in the car and loped toward the arena. He bought two beers from the vendor and headed toward the lower bowl. The place was packed. Paul wasn't surprised. After all, Shaq and the Lakers versus Orlando was a game every Magic fan wanted to see…and win.

He located Angelica and made his way toward her. She was turned, talking to a reddish-blond woman seated next to her. Angelica wore slim fitting jeans and a close fitting T-shirt that accentuated the lines of her body.

His body went on alert. This was why he hadn't called her. He needed to be one hundred percent at work and Angelica interfered with his thinking. Getting to know her better was a double-edged sword. She was addicting. His fingers itched with the need to touch her. To caress her thighs and butt. To test the resiliency of the flesh he'd touched only five short days ago.

She glanced up and waved at him. The welcoming smile on her face made him pause. He'd given her nothing and still she treated him as if he'd made her day. He walked down the aisle toward her. "Hey. I didn't think you were going to make it."

"I almost didn't," he said, passing one of the beers to her. She took it then leaned over and dropped a quick kiss on his cheek.

"Thanks," she said, taking a sip of her drink.

"You're welcome," he said. Had he taken a turn into the twilight zone?

She turned back to the game. He sank into his seat. The Magic played their hearts out and beat the Lakers in overtime.

"What a game! I can't wait to see Rand's face tomorrow," Angelica said.

"Lakers fan?" Paul asked.

"As ever. And he likes to gloat. Is that a male thing?"

Paul shrugged. He knew it was a male thing but

there was no way he was admitting it to Angelica. The crowd slowly emptied out of the arena. Angelica remained in her seat.

"You ready to go?" he asked.

"I like to wait until the crowd is gone. I can't stand being crammed in a throng of people."

Paul relaxed in his seat, finishing his beer. "Was the first half good?"

Setting her cup by her feet, she clasped her fingers together and turned sideways to face him. "Yes, you missed a heck of a game."

Again he wished he could know what was in her mind. No emotions shone from her eyes. And though she smiled, he wasn't sure that she was happy with him. "I know. Sorry."

"No problem. Next time I expect better results," she said.

"Next time?"

"I'm hoping this will be the first of many dates for us."

"I need more than a few hours' notice. Work will always be important."

"I understand. I was kind of nervous. I've never asked a man out before."

"Once again I'm your first?" he asked.

"Get that twinkle out of your eye. While I was sitting here by myself I was reminded there are other fish in the sea."

"Point taken. But this meeting was crucial to Tarron's future and mine."

"You're not the only person who can attend a meeting."

"Are you trying to tell me I'm not as important to Tarron as I believe I am?" he asked.

"I'd never suggest such a thing."

"Good. Because I don't think my ego could stand the blow. Did you eat?"

"I had some popcorn."

"Want to grab some dinner?"

"Didn't you just come from a dinner meeting?"

"Yes, but I didn't really eat."

"Then I'd like that."

The noise from the game still reverberated in his head. The last thing he wanted was to fight the crowds of after-gamers to find a table at a mediocre restaurant on Church Street. And honestly he wanted to see Angelica in his house.

"Do you mind if I order takeout and we eat at my place? I have a nice view of Lake Butler."

"Okay," she said.

He held his hand out and was relieved when she clasped his hand. He led her down the aisle and out of the arena feeling as if something had changed but not sure he could identify what it was.

Angelica wasn't sure what had happened but she'd had a moment of realization as she'd waited for Paul. If he didn't show up it wasn't a reflection on her. She could control her own happiness. She'd made a vow then and there to enjoy her time with Paul.

She wouldn't worry over every meeting and second she spent with him. If he showed up she'd fill the time they had together with every bit of caring she'd been storing up since Roger had died.

But when she followed him to his apartment for dinner, she wasn't sure she'd made the right choice. She was in uncharted waters here. Floundering on her skiff, it was her nightmare situation on land.

The take-out van was waiting by the entrance of the condo complex. Paul parked his car and approached the man. He returned a few minutes later with a fragrant bag. ''Ready for dinner?''

''It smells delicious.''

''Do you like Thai?''

''Love it. Where'd you order from?''

''Tasty Thai.''

''God, I love that place!'' It was a hole in the wall that you'd never expect to have great food.

''Good,'' he said.

She followed him toward the entrance and into his condo. She wished once he'd show her more of what he was feeling. But he never did. And she was honest enough to admit that she wasn't going to be able to pour out her affection on someone who couldn't at least try to meet her halfway.

His apartment smelled like coffee and fragrant Cuban cigars. The kind her father liked to sneak when her mom went shopping. She relaxed in the darkened entryway.

''Can you turn on the light? It's on your right.''

Angelica reached out and flipped the switch. A

rattan armoire sat on one side of the large foyer. Paul tossed his keys in a large, brown wooden bowl with African-style designs on the inside. Next to the bowl was a black-and-white photo of Paul as a boy and a tall, blond girl.

"Who's the girl?"

"Layne, my sister."

"Do you see her often?"

"Not really. She lives in Maine."

"I have two sisters. I talk to them every day."

Paul said nothing just started down the hallway. He flicked on lights as they progressed, revealing the warmth of his home. Trying not to be hurt by the fact that he didn't want to discuss family with her, she observed his place instead.

The furnishings reflected that someone successful lived there, just as she'd expected. There was also warmth and a homey feeling that she hadn't. Forties-style leather chairs and a steamer trunk dominated the living room. A one-of-a-kind oil painting was hung over the fireplace.

Angelica wanted to take off her shoes and feel the Persian rug under her bare toes. She wanted to sit in the big leather recliner that, if the pile of books and newspapers was any indication, was Paul's usual place to sit and relax.

She wanted to surround herself in his place and find a way under his skin. He finally stopped in the kitchen that was dominated by a large butcher-block island that doubled as a casual kitchen dining table.

"I forgot about your water thing so why don't we eat in here?"

She hadn't. It touched her that he'd remembered, but she told herself not to read too much into it. He was used to dealing in details. She would have tested herself again by sitting so close to the water and trying to eat.

"Thanks," she said.

Paul pulled a bottle of wine from the built-in wine rack and opened it to let it breathe. He moved with effortless masculine grace that made her glad she was a woman. And as she started to help him out there was no symmetry to their movements. It was obvious they were both unused to having someone else in the kitchen with them.

She turned quickly and bumped into Paul. His arms came around her, steadying her. His chest was hard against her arms that she had crossed over her breasts holding the plates. She glanced up at him.

His face was so close she felt the humid warmth of his breath with each exhalation. "Sorry."

"My fault," she said, trying to gather her scattered wits. Dang it, whenever he touched her she forgot to think.

He didn't release her and she made no move to break the contact with him. He maneuvered one hand between their bodies and took the plates from her, setting them on the countertop. Then tugged her closer in his embrace.

"I've been wanting to do this since you gave me that brotherly peck on the cheek at the game."

She raised her eyebrows. "I don't think of you as a brother."

"Good," he said, lowering his head.

His mouth was a remembered treat. Warm and masculine, coaxing yet conquering. He forced her to respond and anchored her firmly in the present. In the now. She'd never really lived in the moment before Paul. When he touched her she forgot about the past, forgot about the present. Just remembered Paul and his electric touch.

His hands slid down her back and over her rump covered by her jeans. She loved these jeans because they were tight without being indecent and made her feel sexy when she wore them. She knew that Paul liked them too. He traced the seam of her jeans as his mouth moved on hers, making her feel like the most desirable woman in the world.

She grasped his shoulders, feeling his heat through the thin barrier of his dress shirt. She tested her nails against his muscled arms and felt them clench in response. A wave of craving swept through her. Her nipples hardened against the soft cotton of her T-shirt. She wanted to rub her breasts against his chest and relieve the ache. The urge was stronger than anything she'd ever experienced.

She leaned forward, their lower bodies melded together. Paul's erection brushed against her groin. She moaned, wanting a deeper touch, another touch, more of Paul.

He groaned deep in his throat, the sound distinctly male. His grip on her backside changed and his fingers clenched against her and he rubbed himself slowly against the part of her that needed him.

Tilting her head back she undulated against his body, letting the moment take control. He was solid and strong, everything that she wasn't. Their bodies celebrated those differences and demanded that they do something about it.

Paul's mouth found her neck, his kisses were long and drugging on her neck and then he found her pulse and suckled her skin there. The contact sent a tingle from her neck to her groin and she felt on the edge of orgasm. On the edge of something totally foreign and a part of her was scared of this moment.

But this was the new Angelica, ready to take on the world. Paul lifted her and walked to the butcher-block island, setting her on the countertop and stepping between her legs. His mouth settled on her nipple and he suckled her.

She moaned deep in her throat and her fingers burrowed in his hair, holding his head to her. He transferred his magic touch to her other breast, lavishing his attention on it. She undulated against him and he moved one hand between their bodies, rubbing at her pleasure center through the seam of her jeans. She felt herself melting.

"Paul," she said.

"That's it, Angel. Let me help you fly," he said.

He bent again to her breast and as he suckled there, he touched her a little harder through the fabric of her jeans. The contact sent her over the edge, she moved her hips fiercely against him.

Her body clenched and she shivered in his arms, calling his name. She fell forward, resting her head against his shoulder. Paul held her until the trembles stopped racing through her body.

Oh my God. What had happened? Where had that wanton creature come from? She wasn't sure what to do next. She stiffened. Was there a graceful way to remove your legs from the hips of a man who'd just given you your first orgasm in years? Etiquette books, at least the ones she'd read, had never covered this.

She closed her eyes and held on to Paul, refusing to turn her head and look at him.

"I'm not going to disappear," he said.

"I know. I was hoping you would."

"Angel, look at me," he said.

She didn't want to. But she'd never been a coward, so she lifted herself up and met his gaze. For once there was fire instead of ice in his gaze and she felt as if she could glimpse the inner man she so desperately wanted to release.

But then he sighed and rubbed his forehead. And she knew postcoital bliss wasn't in the cards for her.

Eight

Paul had never come so close to the edge before. He still ached to bury himself in Angelica's body and never leave. She made him feel warm in his soul and he'd been cold for too long. However, her body language, and the fact that she'd all but tried to disappear, told him she wasn't ready for that.

Though he wasn't a masochist, he wasn't going to push her. He knew that her barriers were flimsy now and he could probably have the victory of her body but it would be short-lived. Once he got Angelica in his bed, he planned to keep her there for a long time.

Her nipples still made turgid points against her shirt. Her skin was still flushed and her lips were red. He hadn't taken near enough time with her mouth. He needed more.

He decided to do the gentlemanly thing, step back from between those long incredible legs of hers, brush his fingers along her jaw. If their mouths touched again he wasn't sure he could retreat. He did so reluctantly.

He knew he should say something to break the mood but he wasn't built that way. Had never seduced a woman with soft words. All of his liaisons had been sexual in nature with women who'd been looking for the same thing.

Angelica was different. In ways he was only now beginning to notice. Ways that made him feel aeons too hard for her. And he didn't like that. In business they were well matched so it followed that they should be equals on this level as well.

But they weren't. He was still rock-hard and it was all he could do not to give in to his basic instincts and take what she had offered, albeit unconsciously, a few moments ago. Paul prided himself on his control. In fact, he had been so successful in life because of his control.

He lifted her off the countertop. She rubbed her hands down her legs and bit her lip. Dammit, man, think of something to say. Her eyes were huge orbs giving her appearance a vulnerability she didn't usually project. Feeling awkward and totally inept, he turned back to the counter and retrieved the plates.

"Paul?" she asked.

"Yes?" He set down the plates and started dishing up food. The pungent scents of ginger and curry filled the air but didn't blunt the smell of Angelica that was still in his head. Every breath he took he felt as if he pulled her essence deeper and deeper into his soul.

And he didn't want her in there.

"Are we going to pretend it didn't happen?" she asked. There was something slightly defensive about her words. He realized she must feel awkward too. That she'd been the one to go over so beautifully in his arms and that was a very vulnerable moment. One that he hadn't shared.

Pretending it didn't happen wasn't going to work. They both knew it had and he was a realist. "I don't think either of us will be able to forget it."

"I know I won't."

"But now isn't the time for a postmortem," he said.

"Want to talk about what you're feeling?" she asked.

Hell, no. "Let's eat. The food's already getting cold."

"If you can't talk to me about your emotions we're never going to make any progress. I can't be the only one contributing affection here."

He knew what she wanted for him. He sensed that if he confessed some emotional vulnerability maybe in her eyes things would be more equal between them. Maybe then she wouldn't be the only vulnerable one, but he wasn't about to let her glimpse beneath his armor. Especially not now.

"Angel, the only thing I can think about right now is the fact that I'm still hard and the only way I want to change that is to bury myself hilt-deep in your sweet body.

"Unless I'm mistaken, that isn't where you want to go next, so let's eat." He knew he'd said too much and the wrong things.

She went still and her face flushed. He felt like a bastard. He knew he should have kept his mouth shut. This was a prime example of why he didn't date women who believed in love.

"I'm not sure how to respond to that," she said carefully.

"I'm just a little edgy," he said. And he was. There were only two things that might take the edge off. The first he'd just described to her, the second was a long mind-numbing run.

"I'm sorry. Listen, I think I'll just leave."

She gathered her purse from the floor where he must have knocked it when he'd lifted her to the countertop. She pivoted quickly without a backward look.

"Angelica, wait."

She stopped but didn't turn around. He had a keen fear that one more wrong move and he'd never see her again. He didn't know how to proceed.

"I can be a bastard sometimes. I told you I'm not the kind of guy who knows the right things to say."

Slowly she pivoted to face him. And the look on her face wasn't one of sympathy. "Don't cop out on me now, Paul. You've always been honest with me.''

''What?'' He kept forgetting that just because she looked like his pocket angel she wasn't putty in his hands.

''I mean you know that wasn't what I wanted to hear. You were angry and you lashed out.''

''I am angry.''

She nodded.

''But not at you.''

She closed the gap between them. With each step she took toward him, his heart beat quicker and he wanted to back away, to run.

''Why?'' she asked.

''Because I never lose control.''

''Nobody's perfect, Paul. Not even you.''

He shrugged. He knew that, but usually his control was unbreakable. The way he imagined himself to be most of the time. Why then did this curvy little angel keep reminding him that he might be human after all?

From the moment she'd left his apartment ten days earlier, Angelica had thought of nothing but her last words to Paul. She'd supervised the cleaning of his apartment though her staff hadn't really needed her there to get the job done.

She'd talked to Paul's secretary every day, making arrangements for dry cleaning and carpet cleaning. Taking care of the details of his personal life as a wife would. And for the first time since she started her business she wished she were really a wife—his wife.

That scared her because Paul had proven he wasn't interested in any kind of relationship that had emotions attached to it. Even their near-sexual encounter had been tinged with the same coolness he treated encounters with other people.

She shook her head. Today wasn't a day for worry. Her business was thriving and she'd just signed a new corporate account with Tarron to do all of their training for new hires. These types of accounts were the backbone of her business.

It was a pretty spring day and she had the blinds open on her windows. She had a nice view of the parking lot and the flower beds that bordered the building on either side. The intercom buzzed. "Yes?"

"Mr. Sterling, line two," Kelly said.

"Thanks, Kel. Bring me the contract for Tarron when you're done typing it."

"No problem, boss lady," Kelly said, disconnecting the line.

"Paul?" She braced herself for the silky sound of his voice.

"Hello, Angel."

The deep sound rolled over her like mink on her skin. She wished she knew what his naked skin would feel like on hers. Funny how they'd been so intimate yet still so many barriers remained between them. "How was London?"

"Busy. I have a dilemma."

Paul was obviously in his work mode at the moment. No time for chitchat.

"Can I help?" she asked. She could be professional, too. In fact, she barely remembered that the last time she'd seen him his hair had been rumpled from her fingers.

"I hope so. I know I used my second date for domestic service, but I have a dinner tonight with Tom and he asked me to bring a date."

She didn't see the problem. "You have a third date."

"I'm going to need you for the board of directors meeting at the beginning of May," he said.

Well, that made things a little clearer. Obviously he didn't want to presume on their personal relationship, which consisted of that one date. "That's okay. I'll go."

"We need to make an addendum to the contract we have. I'll bring a check to cover this change."

"Money is handled through accounting, so don't bring a check. We'll invoice you. I thought we were kind of dating," she said, not sure why he was being such a stickler about this point. And she wasn't taking a check from him before she went out on a date. It would be too strange.

"We are. But this is business."

"I don't understand." Although a part of her thought she did. For Paul life was either work or not—and never the twain shall meet.

"I wouldn't bring just any woman to this kind of dinner. I need you as the president of Corporate

Spouses. Not Angelica Leone.'' His words sounded logical but she had the sensation of stepping through the looking glass. Nothing was normal here.

"I don't compartmentalize my life the way you do." She'd never been able to. Even after Roger had died and she knew life would be easier if she just stopped caring about those around her, she couldn't. She needed all of her life to be intertwined. Her business and personal lives were halves of the same whole.

"Still, this is business. If we were dating I wouldn't have invited you."

She shouldn't be surprised by remarks like that but she had to admit she was. "You sure do know how to make a girl feel good."

"I'm not telling you anything new. You are the best at what you do." She heard the truth in his words. Paul wasn't going to sugarcoat things.

"I meant the part about if we were dating."

"Oh. That's to be expected. Don't take it personally."

"There's no other way to take it."

"Sure there is. This is a great opportunity for your company." Again with his logic.

"I don't even want to know what you mean by that."

"You can get some exposure to Tom and show him what your company can do."

"I already have a contract with Tarron," she said. She'd worked hard to get the agreement.

"Great. Then this will prove to Tom he was right to offer you one."

"There are other things in life besides business."

"I want you to have a reason to be there with me, Angel," he said. She sensed that he was trying to tell her something without saying the words. She wished they were face-to-face so she could see his body language.

"Just being with you would be enough for me if you weren't being such a...a...man."

He chuckled. "Hey, I resemble that remark."

"Yes, you do. We don't need a contract to make this workable."

"I'd feel better knowing you were being reimbursed for the evening."

"Fine. I'll have Kelly fax an addendum to Corrine for your signature."

"Now that's the way I like you," he said.

"Professional?" she asked.

"*Agreeable.* I'll pick you up. Say, around six."

"Since it's business I'll meet you there."

"Don't be ridiculous," he said.

"You started it," she said. Real mature, Angelica. For some reason Paul brought out sides to her she hoped she'd buried.

"Good, then I'll finish it tonight at six when I pick you up."

"Are you always this mule-headed?" she asked.

"Usually. See you at six," he said, disconnecting the call.

Angelica hung up the handset and stared at the

top of her desk. Paul's face danced in her mind. Though he'd been stubborn and a tad arrogant, she couldn't wait to see him tonight.

Paul glanced at his watch and knew he'd be in hot water if he showed up late tonight. He had about five minutes to get to Angelica's place and traffic was at a standstill on Highway 50. He reached for his cell phone, dialed Corrine and had her connect him to Angelica's home number.

It rang five times before she picked up. It would be just like her to go to the restaurant when he'd told her he'd pick her up. The fax cover letter she'd sent this afternoon had been cold and to the point. Very un-Angelica.

"Hello?" she answered, breathless.

"It's Paul. I'm running a few minutes late," he said.

"Okay."

Well, for someone who'd made such a big deal about calling she wasn't all that appreciative now. "I thought we could save time by running over a few facts about the Cortells while I'm driving to your place."

"Uh…can you hang on a minute?" she asked.

"Yes."

He heard the phone hit the floor.

"There we go. I was in the middle of dressing when you called."

Immediately, an image of her in black thigh-high hose and a matching bra-and-panty set assailed him.

He knew how she looked in the middle of climax but not how she looked naked. There was something inherently wrong about that. He vowed to rectify that situation and soon. "Tell me you weren't talking to me in your underclothes."

"I wasn't," she said too quickly.

"Too late. The image is already planted in my head." And it wouldn't go away. He hadn't been paying attention and he knew who was to blame.

"Then I won't tell you that I just pulled on my panties," she said.

He slammed on his brakes. Horns honked behind him and a red Mazda swerved to avoid hitting him. "Angel. I'm trying to drive here."

"Did that bother you?" she asked.

He wasn't sure if she was trying to get back at him for their earlier conversation or not but she had an arsenal of weapons that he didn't want her to realize would effectively annihilate him.

"What do you think?" he asked.

"Maybe next time you'll be early," she said.

He chuckled despite the hardening of his groin. She was everything that he liked in a woman. Smart, funny and sexy as hell. She kept him on his toes as no one else ever had.

He even contemplated calling Layne and getting her opinion on how to deal with Angelica but he knew his sister would advise him to follow his heart. And Paul also knew he was the Tin Man missing that organ. Even the Wizard of Oz hadn't been able to help the Tin Man.

"Let's talk business," he said, tired of his own thoughts.

"Yes, let's. How many couples will be at dinner?"

"Six including you and I. Tom and his wife, Chancey, will be there as will three other board members, Steve Jeffers, Marge Thomas and Lou Gennani with their spouses. But the most important guests are the Cortells."

"Who are they?" she asked.

"The Cortells own a small yacht-building company in South Florida. Tom wants to bring them into the Tarron company and is negotiating a friendly buyout. Jeff Cortell is definitely interested but he knows Tom is retiring soon and wants to make sure that the new CEO will keep the traditions of Tarron intact."

He liked that she listened instead of asking a bunch of questions. He would never have taken a date to a dinner like this in the past. Regardless of the fact that he'd have been the only one alone, because he didn't like to have to explain how important the dinner was and the fact that it wasn't really a date but a business meeting. Angelica would know that.

"Is that all?" she asked.

"Yes. I've got a prospectus on Cortell's yacht company if you want to read it on the way to dinner."

"I will. Are you going to be the new CEO?" she asked.

He wasn't sure she'd picked that up. "Officially the board hasn't voted yet. But Tom is pushing for me and frankly I'm the best man for the job."

Silence on the other end. Had he managed to intimidate her? He couldn't believe that he had. But maybe she was thinking that a CEO wouldn't be worth her time. The job was more demanding than his current role.

He didn't want to think about a life without Angelica in it. "You can still sass me, I won't touch your contract with Tarron."

"Ha. I'm not afraid of you."

"You're not?" he asked because he believed that she really was. The woman who'd waited seven years to try to conquer her fear of water wasn't someone who'd easily want to get involved with a man again.

And he knew that despite her bargain with him there was a part of her that she was preserving from him. He didn't blame her. He was doing the same.

"No, because I know what your Achilles' heel is," she said.

He didn't think she really knew what his weakness was. He'd been careful to make sure that he didn't reveal even a hint of it when he was with her. Even their conversation about love had been a smokescreen. But you never knew what slipped out. "What would that be?"

"Women in panties," she said.

"Angel, I'm turning into your driveway right

now. I hope you have more than that on or for once I might forget about business.''

''Is that what it would take?'' she asked, suddenly serious.

He couldn't answer her because the truth was she distracted him in a business suit or in another room. Just knowing she was close by was enough to make him lose focus and he wasn't used to that. He was the man with the plan and that plan didn't involve distractions like Angelica.

Nine

The dinner had been everything Angelica expected and more. Paul was at his best in a social situation. He'd been charming and suave. But also kind and caring, making sure that no one felt left out. Just as they had at the yacht club, they'd functioned well as a couple. Both playing off each other and helping each other.

A sense of rightness filled Angelica as they left the restaurant. Tom's wife, Chancey, was chic and fit and looked years younger than the fifty-eight that she'd confessed to being. Angelica watched the Tarrons leave, liking them even more than she had the first time she'd met them.

Paul's Mercedes appeared next and Angelica decided she wouldn't mention the obvious matchmaking attempts of the Tarrons. Once she was seated in the car, she shivered as the cool leather enveloped her. It had been apparent throughout dinner that the Tarrons considered Paul more than an employee. They considered him family.

And as the evening went on, it became equally apparent that Paul was uncomfortable with the affection they showed him. Did Paul even realize how much they cared for him?

Paul adjusted the air conditioning and turned the radio on low. The sensual stylings of the Dave Matthews Band filled the car. Angelica closed her eyes.

"Mrs. Tarron confessed that she's given up trying to fix you up," Angelica said as Paul steered them out of the parking lot.

He arched one eyebrow at that. "I wish."

Dave sang about the space between two hearts and Angelica looked across the small space separating her and Paul but knew there was really a chasm. One that she might never be able to build a bridge over. One that he might not ever want to cross.

"Why do you let her fix you up?" she asked. It didn't fit with the man she'd come to know.

"She's Tom's wife."

"It's a political thing to keep you in the boss's good graces?"

He shrugged but didn't respond. She watched the road as he got on the expressway. "It started out something like that...she's got a good heart."

They were in foreign territory. So much had

changed between them in the last few weeks. And she was afraid to push harder and drive him away. But she needed more.

"I didn't think you believed in those things," she said.

"Hey, I don't believe in love. Everyone has heart or passion. Her passion is to make sure that everyone has a mate."

"She did mention you were stubborn but I shouldn't let that stand in my way."

"Did you tell her we have a business arrangement?"

"Yes."

"What did she say?"

"Bull hockey. And I have to tell you, hearing those words come out of her mouth was weird."

"That's a Tomism."

"They obviously love each other."

"Your point is?"

"Don't you want what they have?"

"No."

"Why not?"

"Chancey had a double mastectomy last spring. For a while it was touch-and-go and she almost died. Tom lost his way. He couldn't work or eat."

"But now they have each other. I bet Tom doesn't regret a minute of the time he's spent with her."

"What if he'd lost her?"

"He didn't. That is the redemptive quality of love. It pays you back fourfold."

"That works for the pain, too."

"Paul, I can't believe you fear the unknown."

"I don't."

Dave was singing a fast-paced song but she tuned him out. Once and for all, she needed to find out what it was that made Paul tick. She had the feeling that if she ever did unravel the mystery, she'd have the secret to making him love again. To making him shower those around him with affection instead of hiding in the shadows. He'd told her that watching his mother pine after a man who wasn't there had made him wary of loving. But Angelica sensed there was more to it than that.

"What's your passion, Paul?"

He slowed as they approached the toll plaza and then continued through the E-PASS lane.

"Don't say your job. Something not work re-lated."

More silence grew between them and she realized he might not answer her. Maybe she didn't have a right to ask the tough questions. Maybe it was a question he didn't want to answer himself. Maybe he'd decided she wasn't worth the effort and was trying to think of a nice way to tell her to mind her own business.

"My passion is security."

"Like being safe?" she asked. He didn't seem like one of those guys who spent all their spare time in the surveillance store at the mall. If memory served, he didn't have a security alarm system at his condo.

"No. I meant for my life. I guess a better word would be stability."

"Did you have that as a child?" she asked. She remembered him mentioning his mom, but he'd revealed little else about his childhood.

"Until my dad died."

"Oh, Paul."

"Don't feel sorry for me, Angel. I'm successful and have a better lifestyle than most."

"But you don't have anyone to share it with."

"I have my sister."

"Does she share your success?"

"I send her expensive gifts that she could never afford."

"Does that make her happy?"

He said nothing. She knew she'd probed deeper than he'd probably intended to let her. But she couldn't help it. Each layer that Paul revealed drew her deeper and deeper and she craved more.

Before she could ask another question he pulled into her driveway. Angelica looked at the man sitting quietly behind the wheel. Letting the silence build around them. She knew that she couldn't allow him to continue to keep her at arm's length. She knew she couldn't sleep another night if she didn't reach out and pull him to her. She knew that inviting him in for a nightcap was risky, but risk was what her new life was all about.

"Want to come in for a drink?"

He turned toward her. She felt the power of his

gaze in the dark car. Then he turned off the engine and his voice when he spoke was rusty and low.

"Yes, I'd like that."

Angelica's house was a small 1950s-style bungalow in Winter Park. He followed her up the paved brick walkway, the fragrant smell of orange blossoms filling the air. The lights from a neighboring house spilled onto the yard. The night was cast in shadows and Paul knew this was a world he lived comfortably in.

As she fumbled in her bag for her keys, he realized this wasn't her comfort zone. He didn't like the feelings of protectiveness that welled up inside of him. He wasn't the kind of guy who could shelter women. He'd tried it and failed horribly.

"I really enjoyed this evening," she said a little nervously.

Paul realized then that he'd been given someone special in the form of Angelica and he hoped he didn't screw up badly, because something told him his angel wasn't cut out for heartache. She tried her key in the lock but it wouldn't turn.

"What's the problem?" he asked.

"Sticky lock."

"Let me try it," he said.

The lock was stuck but with some gentle coaxing he was able to get it to open. He handed her key back. A soft light had been left on inside and spilled out onto the entryway. Creating a warm glow around Angelica and the night.

For once Paul didn't allow his thoughts to dwell on the pros and cons. He didn't even vaguely come close to thinking of business. All he did was react like a man who'd been alone too long.

He only knew that Angelica had something he wanted very much. Something he'd managed to avoid for a long time. Something he knew he couldn't live without for another day.

"I've been meaning to have that lock fixed," she said, taking the keys from him.

He let go of the keys and grabbed her hand before she could pull away. "I can fix it for you."

He caressed her knuckles with his thumb, enjoying the sensation of smooth skin against his. She always made him feel very big and very masculine. Right now, with high heels on, she barely topped his shoulder. When he'd held her in his arms in his kitchen she'd fit there perfectly as if made for him.

"I don't want to be a bother," she said.

He wondered if she was unaffected by his touch, but the fine trembling of her arm let him know that she wasn't. He leaned closer to her. Intentionally invading her personal space. Her pupils dilated and she parted her lips.

"You aren't a bother."

She licked her bottom lip and he tracked the movement with his eyes. She had the sweetest-looking mouth. He didn't think he'd ever get enough of her no matter how many times he tasted her. Lowering his head toward hers he let his breath brush across her mouth. She shivered again and swayed slightly toward him.

Her breasts brushed his chest and he felt the pebbled surface of her nipples against him. He was glad he'd left his jacket in the car. He slid his free hand around her back and anchored her to him. A soft sigh escaped her and she nestled closer until her breasts rested against his chest.

He wished they were both naked. He longed to feel the soft weight of her against him. To luxuriate in the sensation of flesh-to-flesh. He hardened in a rush and his blood started to flow heavily throughout his body, making him feel alive.

"What are you doing, Paul?" she asked breathlessly, rocking her hips against his erection.

"Getting ready to kiss you," he said, running his tongue along that full bottom lip of hers.

"It takes preparation?" she asked, returning the favor. Her tongue felt warm and curious against his mouth.

"Everything worth doing right does," he said. This time he suckled her lower lip, using his teeth in a gentle grip to hold her still as he sampled her the way he would a delectable ripe strawberry.

"You definitely know what you're doing," she said. Her voice was breathless, her cheeks flushed and her breasts brushed him with each deep breath she took.

"I've barely started, Angel," he said, returning this time to sample the delights of her mouth. She tilted her head to grant him access. Instead of storming her gates he eased through them. Taking his time and enjoying the unique taste that was Angelica.

The Pinot Grigio they'd had with dinner lingered in her mouth but the essence he sought was that of his angel. That was the flavor he was addicted to. Last night he'd woken in the middle of the night hungering for her.

She moaned and undulated against him. He knew that tonight he couldn't be noble and walk away. He knew that if he had even a slim chance of retaining the title of hero, he had to give her an option. He knew that time was running out for both of them.

They couldn't continue to see each other at work and not take things to the next level. Tacitly she'd agreed to this, he reminded himself. But he knew that she hadn't agreed to seduction.

"Angel, if we don't stop now we aren't going to get to that drink you invited me in for," he said. Damn, he was noble and heroic. Though his groin ached and he hadn't set her free, he felt good for doing the right thing.

"Are you really thirsty?" she asked.

"Hell, no."

She stepped back and he feared he'd said the wrong thing. He always managed to where women were concerned. Then she took his hand.

"Come into my bedroom," she said.

He followed her into her house, kicked the door closed and stopped her before she could lead him to her bedroom. He needed to taste her again. To remind himself that she was real. That she was solid and for tonight at least—his.

Angelica's senses were overwhelmed with Paul. She forgot about caring and affection. Forgot about the pain that came with becoming involved with a man. Forgot about everything except the taste and feel of him against her.

Although her house was dark, she knew it by heart. It was her sanctuary. The one place that she retreated to whenever she was overwhelmed by her business and her family. A part of her felt a little vulnerable at the thought of Paul seeing the one place where she revealed her true self.

For all that Paul professed to not care about those around him, he was very perceptive. But the quiet strength in Paul's arms around her allayed those fears. She didn't evaluate that too closely, not wanting reality to intrude on this evening.

The remembered feel of him didn't do justice to the reality. He overwhelmed her senses, making her long to cradle him in her arms and never let go. The impulse was laced with sensuality but also with a deep need to shelter this man who was so strong yet had a hidden vulnerability that she was only just beginning to understand.

Paul caressed her arm and her body clenched— heat flooded her center. Her heart beat quicker and quicker and she feared he'd hear it and know her inner secrets. Know that she craved the physical release he'd given her. Know that she needed something from him that she'd never needed before.

He'd pulled her to a stop in the middle of her living room. She didn't know what to do next. Had never slept with any man except her husband and she was woefully out of practice.

"Changed your mind about that drink?" she asked. Did she even have anything she could serve? Unlike Paul she didn't have a chilled-wine rack. Hers consisted of a metal rack in the pantry.

He brushed his lips against the inside of her wrist. Electric pulses spread from where his mouth touched her flesh throughout her body. "No."

She wished he weren't so miserly with his words. She wanted to tug him down the hall to her bedroom and get back to the incredible feelings he generated. "Paul, I'm flying blind here. Help me out."

His mouth moved up her arm, biting lightly against the tender flesh of her inner arm. Her nipples tightened even more, aching for his mouth on them. "I just wanted to take our time. Last time..."

She blushed and was glad for the darkness. If it weren't for his mouth on her arm, she would have bolted but she remained rooted to him. Last time she'd come so quickly. Had it been too fast? "I'm sorry."

"What are you sorry about?" he asked, lifting his head. Her arm was chilled without the warmth of his mouth.

She was almost too embarrassed to speak but she was a new woman. *Be bold and courageous.* Just the right woman for this man. "Being too fast last time."

He chuckled and pulled her into his arms. Dropping kisses on her face and neck. "Angel, you were just right."

"What did you mean?" she asked. She couldn't think when he touched her there. Sparks shot straight to her groin, making her crave him in the most intimate way.

"Where's your bedroom?" he asked.

"Back there," she said with a gesture.

He swept her into his arms and started toward the back of her house. The light from the hallway and the quarter moon provided a romantic backdrop for them. Her bedroom was feminine and frilly and when Paul hit the wall switch she realized he looked out of place there.

He settled her in the center of the queen-size bed on the fluffy goose-down comforter. He removed her shoes and tossed them toward the closet door. He kicked off his own shoes and toed off his socks. When he reached for his belt buckle she swallowed.

She sat up, thinking she should do something other than just watch him strip. But there was a part of her that wanted to see him do just that. The only thing that made her leave the bed was the fact that he might expect her to stand in front of him and take off her clothes.

"Stay there," he said.

"I..."

"Just relax. I'll take care of everything."

"Paul, I think you should know it's been a long time since I've done this."

"Are you trying to tell me you've changed your mind?"

"No. Only that I'm out of practice."

"We've got all night. We'll take our time," he said. He tossed his belt near his shoes, climbing onto her bed. He pushed her backward with his chest until she reclined on the pillows piled against the headboard. His mouth met hers.

His kiss made all of her thoughts disappear. His tongue swept into her mouth and rekindled fires that had banked. His hands slid down her body, expertly finding the side zipper of her dress. He opened her dress and the first touch of his fingers against her skin made gooseflesh break out on her body.

His hands were hot and large. They roamed under her dress, coming close to her aching breasts but not touching them. She moved restlessly on the bed trying to get him to touch her where she needed him the most. But he wouldn't be rushed.

His mouth left hers to travel down her neck, biting and nipping lightly at her pulse point. She moaned again. Helpless to do anything but receive the pleasure he gave her.

He swept her loosened bodice down her arms. She lifted her hips so he could slide her dress off. The bright overhead light made her feel exposed in her lace bra, matching panties and thigh-high hose. Especially when Paul crouched on his knees and just stared at her.

She crossed her arms over her breasts. Her nipples were aching little points and her own touch made her shiver. She clenched her thighs together as his gaze swept down her body.

"Beautiful," he said. "But too tense."

"I can't relax."

"Okay don't relax, just enjoy."

"How?"

"Uncross your arms," he said.

She did as he asked. But wasn't sure where to put them. Nervously moving them from her side to her head.

"Lace your fingers together and place your head on them," he ordered. Something about his tone commanded her to obey.

He leaned forward, his breath brushing the aching tip of her left breast. She arched her back trying to brush against his lips but he was already there. His mouth hot and wet on her. Biting gently then suckling her fiercely. She couldn't leave her hands behind her head. Instead she held him to her. His thick hair a sensuous treat for her fingers. She rubbed her fingers against his scalp and he suckled more strongly.

He transferred his attention to her right breast and the stimulation of his mouth against the lace was almost more than she could bear. Each tug of his lips against her nipple brought an answering clenching deep in her core. She lifted her hips against him.

His erection was hard against her. Just the pressure she needed. She continued to arch against him.

Sliding her hands down his back. The cloth of his shirt frustrated her. She needed to feel the bunch of his muscles beneath her fingers.

She unbuttoned the front of his shirt. His chest was dusted with a light matting of dark curling hair. She slid her fingers through it. Paul braced himself on his elbows over her. She caressed his pectorals and the six-pack of his ribs and abdomen. He was masculine beauty and he called to everything feminine inside of her.

"I missed touching you the last time," she said quietly.

"Touch me now," he said.

She couldn't have resisted his invitation for anything. She started at his neck. His pulse beat strongly under her fingers. She slid them down his chest, seeking out the brown nipples. His quick intake of breath told her he liked her touch there.

She lowered her head and dropped soft kisses on his neck and shoulder. She remembered the way he'd bitten her neck and did the same to him. He shuddered under her touch and his pulse started to race. Emboldened by his response, she slid her mouth down his chest and teased his nipple.

He groaned, rolling to his back and taking her with him. He held her head to his chest. She continued tasting and kissing him. His taste was slightly salty. She knew she'd never forget him or this night.

She moved down his abs to his stomach. It was hard and when her mouth came close to his trousers she felt him enlarge even more. She reached for the button of his pants, but he stopped her.

"Not yet," he said, rolling her back beneath him.

He shrugged out of his shirt and unfastened her bra, tossing them both on the floor. He leaned over her, rubbing his chest to hers. Sensations spread throughout her and she knew she couldn't wait much longer for him. Intentionally she arched against the bulge in his trousers.

He groaned deep in his throat. His hands slid down her sides, grasping her hips, and tilted her toward his lower body. His entire body moved over hers, caressing her and making her squirm to get closer to him.

"I need more," she said.

"So do I," he said.

He stood. Taking a condom from his pocket, he handed it to her. He dropped his pants and stepped out of his briefs. He stood before her naked and ready. And she'd never felt more wanted. More womanly than she did at that moment.

She slid her panties down her legs and kicked them off the bed. He stopped her when she reached for her hose, intending to remove them.

"I like the sight of you in just those," he said.

She smiled at him, feeling much as she imagined Eve had the first time Adam had looked at her with lust in his eyes. "Are you only looking?"

"Hell, no."

He rejoined her on the bed, sheathing himself with the condom. She opened her legs to make a place for him but instead of moving over her, he crouched beside her. He caressed her from head to heels and back again. Lingering at her breasts and the warmth in her center. He parted her gently and caressed the flesh he'd revealed. She arched toward him and felt her climax coming quickly.

"Not without you," she said between panting breaths.

"Once for me. Once with me," he said.

He leaned over and suckled her breasts again. All the while his hand kept up its maddening rhythm. He shifted his touch of her most feminine flesh. His thumb caressing the nub that was the core of her desire and inserting two fingers into her body.

She screamed at the intrusion, her entire body clenching around him as she exploded in climax. He slid over her, his chest crushing her breasts, his masculine flesh seeking entrance into her body that still rumbled with the aftershocks of the orgasm he'd just given her.

"Now?" he asked.

"Now," she said. She wrapped her legs around his hips as he slid deep into her.

He was larger than she'd expected him to be, filling her completely. He paused, letting her adjust, and then started to thrust. She felt the tingles of extreme arousal building in her again and she tightened around him. He clenched her buttocks, angling her hips for deeper entry, and thrust strongly into her.

Everything tensed in her body and she moaned as

she felt her climax again. He caressed her neck with his mouth, biting lightly and then with a harsh groan he came. He shuddered and she held him to her. They stayed locked together until the sweat had dried on their bodies.

Saying nothing, he left the bed to dispose of the condom. Angelica slid beneath the covers, unsure what to expect next, but when Paul returned he shut off the lights and joined her in bed. Angelica tried not to paint Paul as her hero. As the one man she'd been waiting for, but as he held her through the night it was hard not to.

Ten

Paul had never spent the night in a woman's bed. He usually left after the act was finished. Her even breathing told him she was sleeping yet still he didn't want to leave Angelica's arms. That fact alone should have driven him from this feminine boudoir faster than the hounds of Hades.

But he felt anchored to her bed, unable to move from the sweet temptation she offered. Though he knew that affection was the path to destruction for him. Had seen firsthand the way that emotion had destroyed his mother. And although Angelica enchanted him, he knew the emotion wouldn't last.

Tonight she'd been the embodiment of everything he'd secretly longed for in a woman. Her sexiness and shyness had called to everything male in him.

Her intelligence and sassiness turned him on. And her caring made him want to be a better man than he was.

The kind of man she'd want to stay by her side. He felt inadequate to be that man. Felt chained by the soft arms that held him close to her naked form. Felt wrapped in something ethereal and the logical part of him hated that.

He glanced at the clock: *2:00 a.m.* There was still time for him to slip from her bed and escape. But when he started to pull away, she nestled back against him. Her buttocks cradling his hardening erection.

He groaned deep in his throat and she undulated against him. Unable to help himself, he slid one arm under her body to caress her breasts. Her nipples hardened under his fingers and he plucked delicately at them. Her hips rocked against him and she murmured in her sleep.

Tightening the bonds she'd placed around him. What bonds? This was nothing more than sex. He wasn't staying the night here. He was leaving.

But he knew he wasn't. Instead he bent toward her, brushed the hair from the side of her face and kissed her. Sliding his mouth down to her neck and nipping gently at the flesh there. Goose pimples spread down her arm and she moaned again.

More asleep than awake she responded to him instinctively and that rocked his world. He didn't analyze it but tucked it away for further examination. His hands swept down her body and pulled her more closely to him.

Knowing he should let her sleep, but unable to help himself when he felt the humid warmth of her. She called him the way the Sirens had lured sailors for centuries. Her skin was a sweet temptation he couldn't resist.

One of her hands slid between their bodies to clasp his masculine flesh. He groaned and didn't know if he could wait. Her touch was heaven and hell combined. He wanted more of it but each tightening of her fingers, each stroke of her hand, brought him closer to the edge.

"Is it morning?" she asked. She let go of him and turned her head on the pillow.

"Not quite," he muttered. Her lips beckoned and he kissed her. Long, hard and deep with all the passion inside him. It was the way he wanted to take her.

"Do you mind?" he asked, lifting her leg back over his thighs and nestling himself firmly against her warmth. He nudged against her core.

"Please," she said breathlessly.

He searched for his pants with his free arm, pulled another condom from the pocket. He slid away from her and sheathed himself quickly. She started to roll to her back but he stopped her.

He didn't want to see her face when he made love to her again. She'd already seeped into areas of his soul where he didn't want her. Seeing her eyes, watching her come apart for him was adding to the connection he wanted to ignore.

"Let's try something different this time."

She let him maneuver her on the bed. Again he lifted her thigh back over his. This time he placed his hand over her belly and pressed her back against him until not even air could flow between them. He lowered his head to her neck and bit down gently.

She murmured his name. He slid his free hand up to her breasts, plucking at her responsive flesh until her hips moved restlessly against his engorged manhood. He ached to bury himself deep within her but waited because the ache was almost as good as being inside her.

He spread his fingers through the curling hair between her legs, seeking out the nub of her desire. It was swollen with need and as he caressed her it grew beneath his fingers.

"Paul," she gasped breathlessly. "Now."

"Guide me to you," he said.

She reached between her legs, grasped his manhood and placed him at the entrance to her body. "Ready?"

Her hips shifted back toward him and he slipped inside. He continued to pluck at her nipples and suckle her neck. His hand caressed the center of her pleasure in the same rhythm as his hips rocked against her.

He couldn't go deep enough, couldn't get enough of her. Of the soft sounds she made as they moved together.

He rocked harder, needing every bit of her response. Needing everything she had to give because he knew he was giving her everything he had. Everything that he'd always hidden and never revealed to another soul.

It wasn't enough. It was too much. He didn't want it to end so quickly. But his body refused to listen. Refused to slow. He thrust quicker and quicker, deeper and deeper until he felt he could touch her womb. She tightened around him and let out a little scream of release. He lowered his head to her neck and bit delicately as his own climax shook his body.

He'd never come harder. His body jetted its completion and he shuddered under the impact. He tightened his arms around her. Buried his face in her hair. Felt something long chained inside him break loose. That, more than anything, convinced him he had to leave. He waited until her breathing slowed and then carefully disengaged their bodies.

She murmured as he pulled away from her. He dropped a kiss on her forehead and pulled the covers over her naked form. He dropped the condom in the wastebasket and gathered his clothes. Only when he was in his car and driving toward his home did he allow himself to breathe freely, having the feeling of narrowly escaping.

Angelica woke alone. She was naked and ached in unfamiliar places, so she knew she hadn't dreamed Paul's presence in her bed the night before. No note or red rose on her pillow. Nothing left behind but a discarded tie—the one she'd given him as a thank-you gift. But then again she'd known Paul wasn't going to be like Roger.

She swallowed against the feelings swamping her. She'd known it wouldn't be easy. That Paul would fight her every step of the way. But she hadn't realized that it would hurt.

She got out of bed, found her robe behind the closet door and picked up Paul's tie. She set it on her nightstand and stared at herself in the mirror. The woman looking back seemed lost and confused. She couldn't do that again. *Been there done that.*

Was Paul worth this? She searched inside herself as she showered and dressed. Last night had been incredible and she realized as she got in her car and headed toward downtown that she wasn't ready to throw in the towel on Paul Sterling. She knew that she was fighting an uphill battle but it was worth it to her.

She drove to Tarron's downtown office skyscraper and parked in the garage. No walk had ever seemed longer than the one from the elevator down the plush carpeted hallway to Paul's office. She almost chickened out. But the door opened while she was debating and Corrine saw her.

"Hello, Angelica. I don't have you on this morning's schedule. Do you need Paul?" the secretary asked.

"Yes. It won't take long," she said.

Corrine looked at the calendar and then buzzed Paul. "Ms. Leone is here to see you."

There was a pause on the other end. "Send her in."

Angelica smiled at Corrine and walked through the door, unsure what to expect. He's just a man, she thought. Yeah, and you've seen him naked.

This wasn't helping. She wished her inner voice would shut up. But she acknowledged she was not really herself this morning.

"Hello, Angelica," he said, rising from behind his desk to greet her. He gestured to his guest chair and motioned for her to take a seat.

She seated herself and crossed her legs. He avoided her gaze, staring instead at the wall behind her. She bit her lip and wasn't sure where to start.

"What can I do for you?" he asked.

She wondered if he was really going to ignore the fact that he'd spent last night in her arms. "It's more what I can do for you."

"And that is?"

"Just returning your tie," she said, tossing the silk neckwear onto his desk.

He didn't reach for it. His head came up and his eyes met hers. There was no emotion in his gaze. Heck, she'd expected that, but as she really looked at his face, she realized he was tired. It seemed as if he hadn't slept at all after he left her.

His face made her heart ache. She reached across his desk and covered his hand with hers. Taking a deep breath, she asked, "Why did you leave?"

He tugged his hand from under hers and crossed to the window overlooking Orlando. Thrusting his hands deep in his pockets, he searched the horizon for something only he could find, she suspected.

He seemed so alone. She knew that was how he preferred things but she couldn't bear to see him that way. Last night she knew she'd breached some of his barriers. God knew he'd breached hers. And now there was a part of her that would always belong to Paul.

Standing, she went to him. She put her arm around his waist and he stood stiffly by her side, not moving away but not really welcoming her touch either.

The safe thing to do would be to leave now before she let Paul get any farther under her skin. But after last night she knew that she was falling in love with him. There was no way she could leave without trying her damnedest to make him realize that love did exist and it was the best thing to happen between a man and a woman.

"I know this is hard for you...I thought an affair is what you wanted," she said.

He nodded. "It seemed like the perfect solution."

"And it isn't?" she asked.

"Maybe this is how I treat women," he said. Something in his tone made her wonder if that were true. It fit with what he'd told her of himself. That he didn't like emotional entanglements.

"Is it?" she asked.

He glanced down at her. His eyes piercing in their intensity. "Yes."

She realized that he was looking for chastisement

from her. But that wasn't the role she wanted to play with him. She wanted him as her partner, and if he couldn't meet her halfway, she wasn't staying. "Is that all I am to you?"

"No."

"Then why?" she asked.

"Angel, you want something from me that I'm not capable of giving."

"Haven't we had this conversation before?"

He put his hands on her shoulders, turned her to face him. An inch of space separated them, she felt his heat and longed to be closer to him. To stop this conversation and lean her head against his strong chest and rest there.

"Yes, but you keep calling me your hero and there's a part of me that wants to be that for you."

"Oh, Paul."

"Don't say my name like that," he said, pivoting and walking away from her.

"Why not?"

"Because it makes me think that you believe I can be saved."

"Do you need saving?" she asked.

"No, but you do."

"I'm not in danger."

"Yes, you are. Pretend all you want, but sleeping with a man who deserts you isn't your thing."

"Are you planning to leave me again?"

"I don't know."

"We made an agreement. I'm living up to my

end. Now it's your turn to decide if you are going to live up to your end.''

"Let you show me how to care?" he asked.

"Yes."

"I just told you for some reason I can't."

"Maybe you are starting to be fond of me," she said.

"I can't afford to."

"You can't afford not to."

"How do you figure that?"

"There's a deep well of caring inside you. I sensed it right away. Your nature is to protect those around you, especially women."

"I haven't done a very good job with you."

"All I'm asking is that you let me show you what you've been missing," she said.

"I make no promises."

"I'm not asking for any," she said, but in her heart she knew that she hoped for one.

"I'll try."

"That's all I ask," she said. The intercom buzzed and she knew he had work to do. She gathered her things and headed for the door.

"Angel?"

"Yes," she said.

"For what it's worth, I wished I'd stayed."

"Me too," she said and walked out the door.

The last month had passed quickly for Paul. It was almost May and the board of directors meeting was around the corner. After the dinner where they announced the CEO, he would have no contractual agreements with Angelica. But that didn't worry him too much.

He and Angelica had fallen into a routine that fit both of their lives. He'd underestimated the time her business took up. She worked as hard as he did and the woman never seemed to take a rest.

He was meeting her for dinner at Lake Eola. She was big on spending time outdoors and still was battling her fear of water. Last week they'd sat facing the street instead of the lake and she said she'd keep coming to the lake until she could sit at the water's edge and not flinch.

He was actually early for once, having told Tom he had a date with Angelica. Tom had smiled at him and made him leave early. So here he was sitting near the swan boats waiting for a woman who'd done her best to make his life chaos. As much as he resented the feelings she engendered in him, he was helplessly fascinated by her and couldn't stop seeing her.

She'd spent the night at his house twice, which was something he'd never had a woman do before, but with Angelica it had seemed right. He hadn't been able to stay all night at her place and he thought she understood when he left both times, even though he knew he'd hurt her when he'd gone. The very thing he'd hoped not to do.

There was a certain security in Angelica and her caring. She was always there for him. She'd met him at the airport when he'd returned from a weeklong

conference in Los Angeles. She'd sent him a cookie
basket when his team had come in under budget in
the last quarter. She'd fulfilled his secret dreams
without him ever having to say a word.

Slender hands covered his eyes and the scent of
Angelica's perfume surrounded him. "Guess who?"

She'd spoken directly in his ear and heat pooled
in his groin. "My angel?"

She laughed and came around the bench, sitting
on his lap and settling her picnic basket on the seat
next to him. "How'd you know?"

He kissed her instead of answering her playful
question. He'd never met anyone who could make
doing nothing fun, but Angelica did. The kiss was
getting a little too intense for such a public place,
so he pulled back. "We'll finish that later."

She smiled at him but didn't move off his lap.

"Is there a reason why you are sitting here?" he
asked.

"I'm not sure I'm ready for the water," she said,
tucking a strand of hair behind her ear.

"I wish I could make your fear go away," he
said, not sure where the words had come from. He
wished he hadn't spoken.

"Thank you," she said, hugging him close to her.

These quiet tender moments were the ones he really treasured. He'd never admit it to a soul. Not
even to the slender woman holding him now. "Let's
go around to the bandstand and eat there."

He set her on her feet and took the picnic basket
from her. She slid her fingers through his and they

walked slowly away from the water. The path around the lake was busy with walkers and young families. Angelica spread the picnic blanket and Paul wondered if a family was part of Angelica's plan for the future.

Why did he torture himself wondering? He already knew he wasn't her long-haul man. But the thought of her having another man's children made his blood run cold. He wanted her to have everything she wanted in life. At the same time he wished things could stay as they were now. Just the two of them working, dating and making love.

She started pulling containers from the large wicker basket and Paul seated himself next to her. "I brought a bottle of wine."

"Thanks. You have the best wines," she said.

She served him baked chicken, homemade bread and pasta salad. One of the things about Angelica was that she embodied the qualities he associated with womanhood. She was a blend between a domestic goddess and forceful businesswoman. A force to be reckoned with.

He also liked that when she was with him she relaxed her guard. His new feelings for her made leaving her house in the middle of the night so much harder. But he still did it.

"Would you be available for a friendly game of basketball tomorrow night?" she said.

"Against you?" he asked.

"No, playing with me against Rand and Kelly."

"Sure. What are you playing for?"

"Honor."

He arched one eyebrow at her in question.

"Doughnuts on Friday morning."

"Well, for such an honorable cause I'll do my best."

"Thanks. The line at Krispy Kreme is always around the building in the morning and Rand has beat me for the last three weeks."

"Why didn't you mention it sooner?"

"I wanted to win on my own. But since Rand suggested a team sport, I figured you could help me win."

"Of course I will."

"Winning's what you do best."

"A few other things come to mind," he said, tugging her over to him. She settled against him, sipping her wine.

"What are they?"

"Making love to you," he whispered.

"Tell me more," she said.

Feeling like a man on parole, he did. Telling her things he was going to do with her as soon as they left the park. Within a few minutes she was squirming in his arms. They packed up the picnic and raced to his house. The intensity of their lovemaking shattered the illusions Paul had felt safe living within. He now knew that Angelica had entered his danger zone and he had to carefully back away.

Eleven

Angelica dressed for the evening of the board of directors dinner with care. Though it hadn't been made public yet, Paul had been named CEO of Tarron this afternoon. She'd planned a special celebration for the two of them after the dinner and official announcement tonight.

Angelica checked her gown one more time in the mirror. Her hair was upswept, her earrings a smallish pair of diamond studs her parents had given her for her twenty-fifth birthday. Her necklace was a heart-shaped pendant she'd been given for her highschool graduation.

Wearing the jewelry made her feel surrounded by her family's love. She'd splurged on an Oleg Cassini designer dress for the evening. Her strappy sandals were just the right touch.

She glanced around her living room. Candles had been laid on every surface, the CD was queued to play Lena Horne's love songs and on the coffee table was a special gift she'd selected for Paul. Something that would look nice in his new office. Something that would fit with his new life, one that she was sure she'd be a part of.

The last month since they'd become lovers had been a magical time for them. She sensed that he still was uncertain of what he felt for her but was convinced she'd taught him to love.

The doorbell pealed and she hurried through the house. Paul stood in the doorway, dashing in his tuxedo. He was the kind of guy who looked good in formal wear. A thrill zinged through her when she looked at him and knew he was her man.

And he was most definitely her man. Tonight would prove it once and for all. She knew that Paul was the kind of guy who needed to hear about her emotions before he'd feel safe in his.

"Congratulations, Mr. CEO," she said.

"Thanks, Angel."

He dropped a quick kiss on her lips. She slid her arms around his neck and let the warmth of his body seep into her. She'd been so excited when he'd called earlier that she'd wanted to jump through the phone and hug him.

But Paul set her away. "I don't want you to look mussed."

She shrugged. "I can fix my makeup."

"We don't have time right now."

"Why not?" she asked, grabbing her wrap and evening bag from the hall table.

"I can't be late for this," he said.

This was his night, she thought. "Let's go."

Paul took her keys and locked the door for her. He'd fixed the lock a few weeks ago. But he still insisted on locking and unlocking it for her. It made her feel cherished even though she probably shouldn't read too much into the action.

The drive to the Swan Hotel was long during rush hour. Paul fiddled with the radio station, stopping on one of those hard-rock stations he loved. Three Doors Down blared from the speakers. She wondered sometimes if he used the music to keep conversation at the minimum.

Tonight she knew he had to be feeling a million different things. It was the culmination of everything he'd worked for. Yet he was doing all he could to keep her at arm's length.

She reached out and turned down the volume.

He glanced over at her but with the aviator shades he was wearing she couldn't see his eyes. "Sorry."

"No problem. Did you hear the news from Tom this afternoon?"

"Yes. Chancey was there too. She'd baked me a cake."

"Chancey did?" she asked.

"It was the worst cake I've ever had," he said, grinning.

It was obvious he'd been touched by the gesture. Angelica was touched that the Tarrons had gone out of their way for Paul. "How did you feel?"

"Embarrassed."

"Why?"

He shrugged her question aside, turned the radio volume up again. "Hey, I think this is Creed. Did you know they're an Orlando band?"

"Yes, I did," she said, this time turning the radio off.

"Why don't you want to talk about Chancey's cake?" she asked. She knew how much Chancey and Tom cared for Paul. Chancey had spent one morning at the tennis club telling her all about Paul. Regaling her with stories of the hardworking young man he'd been. As if Angelica needed someone to sell her on Paul.

"Are you going to be stubborn about this?" he asked.

"I'm prepared to be."

"Well, I'm only saying this once. It made me feel like I was really part of their family."

"That wasn't so hard, was it?" she asked.

"The jury's still out."

"Being open to emotion is coming more easily, isn't it?"

"Ah, Angel. Don't pin too many hopes on me."

"Don't paint yourself in the dark. You're a better man than you believe you are."

"As long as you believe it, I'll be fine," he said. He coasted to a stop in front of the Swan and the valet opened her door. She slid out of the car, waiting for Paul. He pocketed the claim ticket and put his hand at her back to escort her into the hotel. She felt poised and polished, everything that she'd been the first night she'd met Paul.

But at the same time she was a different woman. She was alive in ways that she hadn't been in a long time. She was fulfilled in a way her company hadn't been able to fill her. She was in love with the man who was showing her his tender side inch by aching inch.

As they entered the ballroom she felt secure that he loved her too. Paul had grown so much in the short time they'd known each other. Telling her about his feelings and Chancey's cake were things he'd never have done three weeks ago. Tonight she'd lay her cards on the table and find out if he really was her knight in shining armor.

For the first time in his life, Paul let the emotions he felt flow through him instead of bottling them up. It was a heady moment that made him question the tenets by which he'd lived his life. The board made their announcement and there was a round of applause that didn't seem forced to him.

Angelica had kissed him and he'd forgotten the speech he'd carefully prepared but it had been worth it. Having her by his side at this announcement was right. He didn't examine it too closely. He knew that she'd become as important to him as his career at Tarron.

The drive home was quiet. Angelica insisted on no rock stations on the radio and he put in a CD of her favorite jazz artist, Miles Davis. She smiled at him and he felt a rush knowing he'd pleased her.

He pulled into her driveway and realized the small cottage house was beginning to feel like home to him. The only thing that would complete it would be a few of his favorite pieces from his condo. He wondered if Angelica would live with him. Planned to ask her tonight. It was a big step for him but with Angelica by his side he felt stronger than he had in the past.

He opened her door, helping her out of the car. Angelica tilted her head back and glanced at the sky. It was a clear night with a full moon and lots of stars.

"Beautiful evening," she said.

"It is," he agreed. He took her hand, leading her up the walkway to her house. She handed him her key and he unlocked the door. Once they stepped into the foyer, she placed her keys in the basket on the table. She set her wrap and purse down as well.

Placing one hand on his breastbone, she leaned up on tiptoe and kissed him.

"Close your eyes," she said.

"Why?" he asked, leaning down to brush his lips down the side of her neck.

"Don't ask questions, just follow orders," she said, stepping away from him.

"Okay," he said.

She left him in the entryway. He felt oddly vulnerable without his sight. He heard the soft clicking of her steps on the hardwood floor as she moved. But had no idea what she was doing. He smelled the match she lit and then the scent of lavender. Then the soulful sounds of Lena Horne filled the room.

Paul tried to relax but as soon as he realized Lena was singing about love, he tensed. He wasn't ready for love. Wasn't ready for Angelica to talk about love.

He flinched when she came up to him. Sliding his jacket off his arms. "Can I open my eyes now?"

"No," she murmured.

She removed his tie, cuff links and the studs holding his shirt together. Then her fingers were on his bare chest and he shivered under her touch. Her nails bit lightly into his skin and he swelled his chest. Wanting her to see him and approve of him.

He started to open his eyes but she must have been watching because her hand covered his. "No peeking. Do I need to blindfold you?"

"Not yet," he said.

She laughed softly, pushing his shirt off his shoulders. He felt odd standing there with only his pants and shoes on. While she wore…what?

"What are you wearing?" he asked.

"Find out," she said.

He reached for her, found the curve of her cheek and her neck. Her skin was so soft that although he longed to know what exactly she had on, he lingered, caressing the hollow between her neck and shoulder. It was one of his favorite spots on her body and he'd never been able to resist dropping kisses there.

Tonight was no different. He bent and kissed her there. Suckling the skin that tasted uniquely of his Angel.

"No kissing. Just touching."

"So there are rules to this?" he asked, sliding his hands over her shoulders that were bare. But the dress she'd had on was strapless, so that told him nothing. He moved both hands in tandem down from her shoulders and encountered only the smoothness of her naked skin. Her breasts were full and weighty as he cupped them.

He opened his eyes. She stood before him in a brief pair of black lace panties, black thigh-high hose and incredibly high heels. He moaned. Incapable of speaking at this moment.

He scooped her up and carried her into the living room that was set for seduction. Candles glowed on every surface. A cashmere throw had been placed in the center of the room in front of the fireplace.

He set her on her feet next to the blanket and removed the pins from her hair. He loved to see the silky length falling around her shoulders. She shook her head and closed her eyes as the mass of curly hair touched her skin.

Paul cupped her head and brought her close to his chest. Her hair was downy soft against his chest. She murmured nonsensical words as she rubbed against him. His groin tightened painfully and he knew tonight wasn't going to be one of the times where passion built slowly between them.

"Sorry, Angel. I can't wait tonight," he said, finding her mouth with his. He thrust his tongue deep inside her and she angled her head, granting him full access. He urged her back on the blanket until she was settled there in front of him. He removed his shoes and socks, impatient to be naked. To feel her flesh against his and bury himself in her hot center.

Unlike the first time they made love, Angelica lay spread before him. Not embarrassed by her semi-nudity but, if the look on her face was any indication, proud of it.

He kicked aside his pants, grabbing a condom from the box she'd left on the table. He sheathed himself and crouched next to her. He removed her panties, hose and heels then bent to suckle her breasts. Her nipples were hard like ripe berries tempting him to remain at her breast for the rest of his days. He bit her lightly. Her back arched, pressing her more fully against him.

He wanted to seduce her in slow and steady movements, to bring her to climax time and again before finally joining her, but his control was gone tonight. When her hand enclosed his manhood, he knew he had to have her—now.

He settled himself between her legs. Using his arms under her thighs, he bent her legs back toward her body, watching her the entire time to make sure she wasn't uncomfortable. He teased himself at her entrance until she shifted her hips, demanding he enter her body.

He did in one strong thrust, going as deep as he could. She moaned in the back of her throat and he set a rhythm that took them both out of their bodies. She never broke eye contact with him, and he knew the moment she went over for him and he followed her in climax.

"Stay with me tonight, Paul," she said.

His heart clenched and his body still shuddered from the release she'd given him. He felt as if he'd been stripped naked in a public place. He pulled out of her warm body and stood, unsure of what to do next.

Angelica got slowly to her feet as Paul grabbed his pants and went into the hall bathroom, presumably to deal with the condom. Oh, God. She wished she'd kept her mouth closed.

But she'd been unable to keep her emotions bottled inside. She'd known for a while now that what she felt for Paul wasn't fleeting but lasting and rooted in the future she sensed the two of them could have. She wanted to tell him of her love but fear held the words inside. She was tired of waiting for Paul to admit his feelings for her. Life was too short to waste time.

She'd felt the shock in him as her words had penetrated his consciousness. She pulled the cashmere throw around her body, wondering how something so right had gone so horribly wrong. He returned a few moments later.

"Angel," he said, holding out his arms.

She went to him and nestled close to his body. His arms around her reassured her as nothing else could. He held her so tightly she thought he was trying to absorb her into his skin. There was something in his stance that warned her he was going to say goodbye. And she couldn't let that happen yet.

"Paul—"

His finger on her lips stopped her words. "No more talking tonight."

Walking around the room, he shut off the CD and blew out the candles. She spotted her gaily wrapped present and the champagne she'd left out.

"We can't go to bed yet," she said.

"Why not?" he asked.

"We have to toast your success and I have a present for you. Sit down."

While he seated himself, she grabbed her satin bathrobe and put it on. She poured the champagne into two flutes, handing one to him.

"To new beginnings," she said.

"New beginnings," he said, touching the tip of his glass to hers and swallowing his champagne. She sensed he didn't really want to toast anything new.

He seemed restless. She shouldn't have asked him to stay. The evening had been going so well up to that point. Sensed that he was trying to find a way to leave gracefully but she wasn't ready to let him leave. Wasn't ready to let him go. He could love her if only he'd give them a chance.

She blinked back the tears in her eyes. Trying to battle the anger that was bubbling up inside of her. Why couldn't he see that life went on whether you loved or not? "Open your present."

He grabbed the package and tore open the wrapping. The brass-framed picture of the two of them stared back at her. It was a candid shot Rand had taken of them after the basketball game last week.

They'd been flushed with victory. Paul held her in his arms, her head was on his shoulder, looking up at him as he'd looked down at her. The moment was frozen in time but she knew in the next instant he'd kissed her. Putting the doubt she'd felt to rest, making her tumble over the edge and fall in love with him.

"Thank you," he said quietly.

He rubbed his chest and set the picture upright on the table in front of them. Watching the photo as if it were a ticking time bomb.

"What's wrong, Paul?" she asked, trying to draw him out as she had in the car about the celebratory cake Chancey Tarron had baked for him.

"I've got to get out of here," he said, standing and gathering his clothes and shoes.

"Will I see you tomorrow?" she asked. They'd initially planned to spend the weekend together.

"I'll call you."

"Haven't we come too far for this kind of brush-off?" she asked.

"It's not a brush-off."

"Then why does it feel like I'll never see you again? I thought we were building a relationship here."

"We are."

"Then stay tonight."

"I can't."

"I need to know something before you leave," she said.

He watched her but didn't speak. The way she felt right now she should just let him go. Why make a mountain out of a molehill? But she also knew that if she didn't stand up for herself she'd be left by love again and this time she wouldn't have fate to blame.

"Do you care for me even a little?" she asked.

"I'm fond of you and I want you like hell on fire."

Inside she crumbled but she knew better than to break down in front of him. Wouldn't let him see that vulnerability that she'd been keeping secret and hoping to share. She could not confess to a love that he didn't share with her. Would never share with her.

"Am I a convenience to you?"

"No, Angel. You are so much more than that. But I refuse to let emotions run my life."

"Do you even have them?" she asked before she could stop herself.

He shrugged into his shirt and pocketed his tie and studs. Then sat on the couch to put on his socks and shoes. "You make me feel more alive than anyone else."

She watched his movements. He never stood still as he talked to her. "That's not a bad thing."

"For me it is. I've told you about my mother. She said that each day without my father was dim. I didn't understand what she meant until I met you, Angel."

Finally he faced her, moving closer. His breath brushing her face with each word he spoke. "Each day with you is an intense explosion of color. You asked me once what I fear and I'm ready to answer you."

She stood still, aware of the tears flowing down her face. Her heart was breaking as she realized just how high the wall guarding Paul's soul was. Just how unreachable his heart was. And just how much he needed her love.

"I'm afraid of waking up one morning and finding out that I can't live without a certain person. Finding that person gone and myself unable to function. That's my fear."

She cupped his face and forced him to look at her. "I'm not going anywhere."

"Life is fragile, you know that."

She knew that better than anyone, but she also knew that life was the risk. "But isn't time spent together better than never knowing love?"

"No," he said.

"Then I guess this is goodbye."

"It doesn't have to be. What we have now is good. Can't we keep going like this?"

"I can't. I want to take you home to meet my family. I want to bring our lives together and I want to someday have children—with you."

"I can't do that."

His words angered her. Most of it was self-directed because he'd never promised her anything else. But a part of it was for him because he wouldn't take a chance on her.

"I never thought I'd say this but you are a coward, Paul Sterling. You hide from life using excuses to protect you from the one thing you fear so much, never realizing that all you are doing is creating a lonely existence."

She was breathing heavy and the tears she'd cried earlier had dried.

"I'm not the only one," he said.

She shook her head. "At least I'm trying."

"Not really. You told me once you are afraid to tempt fate. And instead of doing that, you started a relationship with me that had no foreseeable future."

"I want a future with you."

"On your terms."

"You said it yourself, life is fragile. I want to fill all my days with you now in case..."

"Exactly *in case*. We're the wrong people for each other, Angel."

She couldn't watch him as he walked out the door

and out of her life. Her eyes fell to the torn wrapping and she noticed he'd left the picture behind. The tears she'd refused to shed fell as she realized exactly what she'd given him. And it wasn't love.

Twelve

Paul swung by Einstein Bagels on his way to work Monday morning. He'd had a crappy weekend where he'd vacillated between anger at Angelica and anger at himself. He'd never wanted to hurt her. But that seemed to be the only thing he'd accomplished.

That and wounding himself. Because hurting someone weaker than himself was the one thing he'd always despised. Right now he was heading for the one place where he'd always found solace. Maybe that meant she wasn't necessarily the weak one. Maybe he was.

He entered the office. Corrine was at her desk, working efficiently at her computer. "We need to sync your Palm Pilot because there are some updates to your calendar."

He took his PDA from his pocket and handed it to her. She started working on it. "Congrats on the promotion."

"Thanks, Corrine. Put yourself on the calendar today for thirty minutes. We're going to talk about your future."

"My future?"

"There's always room for you on my team but I don't want to keep you behind this desk if there's something you'd rather be doing."

"Thanks, Paul. I'll think about it."

"There's bagels for the staff in the kitchen."

She nodded.

He entered his office, turned on his computer and then stared out at the Orlando skyline. It's just an ordinary Monday, he reminded himself. But there was nothing ordinary about a day when he wouldn't see Angelica. She's just a woman, he reminded himself. A part of him believed she'd change her mind and come back to him.

They'd been good together and for each other. He'd been working at getting her over her fear of water. She'd been working on helping him interact with people more, be less of a loner but now he knew the truth. No matter how much he interacted with others he'd never change.

"Here's your Palm. I downloaded your 'A' file e-mails, as well. You're expected in the conference room in ten minutes to meet with one of our new corporate partners."

"Thank you," he said, taking his PDA from Corrine and starting down the hall. He checked his calendar as he went. The day was booked solid and that was something. He should be able to keep Angelica out of his mind.

He entered the conference room. Three people sat at one end and he ignored them as he went to get his coffee and took his customary seat in the middle of the table. He glanced again at the people at the end of the table and recognized Rand first.

Hell.

He scanned Kelly's face and met Angelica's chilly eyes. She was still mad. He kissed goodbye any thoughts that she'd be coming back to him when she realized he'd meant what he said.

Tom entered the conference room, sat down next to Paul and started the meeting. The meeting was to hammer out the details of the classes that Corporate Spouses would be teaching at Tarron over the next eighteen months.

"Rand Pearson will be handling this account. He's our specialist in teaching etiquette and business ethics."

"Good. Rand, we'll get Corrine to meet with you and build your classes into our training calendar."

The meeting wrapped up swiftly and as everyone stood to leave, Paul realized that he couldn't let Angelica just walk away.

"Ms. Leone?"

"Yes, Mr. Sterling?"

"Can I have a moment of your time?"

"Rand, Kelly, I'll meet you both downstairs," she said.

Tom left the room and the staff of Corporate Spouses followed him. Alone with Angelica, he was unsure how to proceed. This was the time for all the finesse he'd cultivated over the years. Don't blow it, he warned himself.

"I missed you this weekend," he said.

"You didn't have to."

"I felt I did. Have you thought about what I said?"

"Continuing as we were?"

He nodded.

"I can't."

"I'm giving you all that I have."

"That's why I can't go on. You were right when you said I was afraid to tempt fate."

"Why listen to me now?"

"Because there was a grain of truth in your words, Paul. I didn't trust you to stay with me and didn't trust fate to let me keep you."

"Fate has nothing to do with our relationship. We're two consenting adults in a mature relationship. There's no reason that has to end."

"I need to believe in the future. Not only the ever-present now."

"You're sure?"

She nodded. "And I can't go along like you do, pretending I don't care."

"I never asked you to."

She stared him squarely in the eye. "Yes, you did."

She walked away and this time he knew she'd left his life for good. A part of him wanted to say good riddance. He didn't need the distraction, but deep inside, the man who'd been hoping she was right when she'd said he was her hero returned behind his wall.

Angelica didn't look at Rand or Kelly when she exited the elevator. Only walked straight out into the sunny Florida day, pulling on her sunglasses.

"Are we going to pretend nothing happened in there today?" Rand asked.

"Not now," she said to him.

"Okay, but soon," Rand said.

He was her best friend. If anyone could help her out of this mess it was Rand. But she didn't want out of the mess. She wanted to remember that being alive hurt. That loving was pain. And Rand wouldn't let her wallow in self-pity the way she wanted too.

Kelly said nothing as Rand drove them back to the office. Rand drove a classy BMW that he said enhanced the company image. He thought her car detracted from the image and refused to let her meet clients in her vehicle.

When they entered their building, Angelica hurried to her office and closed the door. She needed to be alone right now. Not talking to a man when she thought they were all insensitive clods.

She hit the intercom button. "Kel, I don't want to be disturbed this morning."

"Sorry, boss lady. Rand is on his way in."

Angelica glanced up as the door opened and Rand walked in. Settling himself in her guest chair, he steepled his fingers over his chest and waited.

"Please, not today."

"I just got volunteered for eighteen months of teaching classes. You owe me something here, kiddo."

"I'll wear Lakers colors to work every time you teach a class."

"Nice, but no-doing. What's up with you?"

"I know we said going into this that we'd always share everything fifty-fifty. You've been a better partner than I could have expected but I can't do fifty-fifty with Tarron."

"Again, I must ask, why?"

"Because I broke the number one rule... Don't get personal with a client."

"Sterling?"

She nodded.

"I could be wrong but from where I stood it looked personal for him too."

"No, it's not. He's not the kind of man who can love a woman."

"Every man can love," Rand said.

"He told me he can't."

"Can't say the words, or can't feel the affection?"

"Both."

"And you believed him?"

"Rand, what are you saying here?"

"I'll tell you a male secret, kiddo."

She leaned across her desk. Rand scooted his chair closer to her. "Men are afraid of women."

"Right."

"Really. You make us examine things we don't like to admit we even have. Like feelings and emotions. Because it ruins the illusion that we're unbreakable."

"Everyone's breakable."

"Yeah, but with men we don't like to admit it."

Rand stood, pausing at the doorway. "I'll teach half the classes, but you've got to do your share. You didn't hide after Roger died. I'm not letting you hide now."

He walked out the door and closed it firmly behind him. Angelica folded her arms on her desk and laid her head down. Rand made sense but she had no idea what to do. She knew that unless she told Paul that she loved him, she couldn't expect him to trust her and do the same.

She had been afraid to tempt fate and love again. But love had blossomed in her heart just the same. And it was time to face Paul again and tell him what she was feeling.

Paul worked through lunch and didn't have time to think until late afternoon. Only then did he acknowledge he'd made the biggest mistake of his life. All day he'd relived the words he'd exchanged with

Angelica. Relived the time he'd spent with her. Relived the moment she'd walked away and he'd let her go.

He realized he was a coward and Angelica had been right to call him one. He'd never be free of her and he never wanted to be.

Picking up the phone, he called his sister. She answered on the first ring. "Layne, it's Paul."

"What's up?" she asked.

"I'm not sure why I called."

"I've got all morning. Dev took the boys out on the boat with him."

"I met a woman, Layne."

"Tell me about her."

"You'd like her. She's kind and caring."

Silence crackled on the line and he knew his sister was waiting for him to elaborate.

"She thinks I'm a hero."

"Really?"

"Not anymore."

"Do you want to be her hero?"

"I think so."

"Then do it."

"It's not that simple. I don't want to be like Mom."

"You could never be like Mom."

"How can I be sure?"

"You are stronger than she is already. She needed someone to make her complete. You are your own man without this woman."

"I'm so much better with her," Paul muttered.

"Then you know what you need to do," Layne said.

He hung up realizing that Layne was right. He needed Angelica in his life. Already she commanded his thoughts and owned his dreams. And if he were honest he'd admit she owned more than that. She owned the heart he'd hidden away for so long.

He only hoped it wasn't too late to win her back. Standing, he left the office.

"Cancel the rest of my day," he told Corrine. "I'm going to find Angelica."

"Paul, there's something really important at five."

"No. Nothing's more important than Angelica."

He left his office realizing the truth of the words. Without Angelica by his side the success he'd found at work was hollow. A light rain fell as he walked across the parking lot. And he saw the sun breaking through the clouds as he drove away from the lot. Knew that it was a sign that he was making the right choice.

He turned onto the road and was sideswiped. He tried to control the spinning of the car, but as he hit the steering wheel and the world went dark, he only hoped he hadn't waited too late for love.

Thirteen

Kelly buzzed the intercom just as Angelica was leaving for the evening. She'd called Corrine and had her schedule Paul for a late meeting so that he'd still be at the office when she arrived. But she had to leave now or she'd be late.

Impatiently she grabbed the phone.

"Make it quick, Kelly."

"It's Corrine. She said it's an emergency."

"Put her through."

"This is Angelica."

"Listen, Paul's been in a car accident. They took him to Orlando Regional Medical Center. I know you were planning to surprise him here."

"Oh my God," Angelica said. The blood rushed

from her body and she felt faint. Damn, she'd tempted fate and lost again.

"Are you still there?" Corrine asked.

"Yes."

"Will you go to the hospital? His family is out of state."

"Sure I'll go. What's his condition?"

"I'm not sure."

When she arrived at ORMC, Paul was in the emergency room. Only by saying she was his fiancée was she allowed down the hall to the curtained room where Paul was seated.

He glanced up when she entered. His forehead was bandaged and a nurse was checking his stats. Angelica wanted to rush to him and cradle him in her arms. She wanted to fall to her knees and thank God that he was okay. But she wanted most of all to tell him of her love.

"Angel, what are you doing here?" he asked.

"Corrine called me."

"And you came."

"I'll always come to you, Paul," she said.

The nurse finished and stood. "I'll be back to put the cast on that arm in a few minutes."

The nurse left them alone and Angelica walked into the room. She wasn't sure where they stood. She'd said some harsh things to him on Friday night and today in his office. He'd been angry when he'd left.

"Angel—"

"Paul—"

"You first," he said.

"Tell me about your accident."

"I was sideswiped leaving the office."

"I thought you had a late meeting."

"I know. But some things are more important than work."

"What things?" she asked.

"I should have said people."

What was he trying to tell her? She remembered Rand's words. Men couldn't talk easily about the things they felt. She settled into the chair next to the bed he was sitting on. She wanted to touch him. Had to fold her hands to keep from reaching out to him.

"Don't you want to know where I was going?"

She nodded.

"I was coming to see you," he said.

"Why?" she asked.

"To remind you that we have a bargain."

"I remember."

"And we made an agreement with one another. I don't want you giving up on me so soon," he said.

"I was coming to tell you that I haven't. I should have trusted you."

"How could you when I was acting like a coward?" he asked.

She stood and leaned over him, cupping his jaw in her hand. "You were never a coward."

"I was and you were the only one brazen enough to call me on it."

"When you fall into a man's arms the first time

you meet him, there's no such thing as pride,'' she said.

He smiled up at her. ''I was coming to tell you something important, Angel.''

She waited.

''I realized that you'd crept into my soul without my noticing it and I can't get you out.''

''I'm sorry. I'll leave.''

He gripped her hand so tightly she couldn't move. ''No. Never leave.''

''I don't understand.''

''Come closer,'' he said.

She bent down so that their faces were only an inch apart.

''I love you,'' he whispered.

''I love you, too,'' she said.

''Will you tempt fate with me? Will you fill my days with color?''

''I will,'' she said.

She left his side only for a few minutes while they applied the cast to his arm. They left the hospital together and went to her house. They spent the rest of the wet May day in her bed where they talked about the future and the past. Talked about dreams and fears. Talked about the love they had for each other and the hopes they had for their life together.

Epilogue

Angelica Leone-Sterling was once again at the charity auction where she'd met her husband the previous February. Corporate Spouses was once again participating in the auction but instead of only women and women-based companies, this year's event was featuring men as well. Rand had lost a Super Bowl bet to Angelica and would be on the auction block tonight.

"Aren't you glad you won't have to catch me tonight?" she said, leaning over to Paul.

"I'm always glad to catch you, Angel."

"Still my hero," she said.

"I'm going to get a drink, can I bring you something?"

"I'm fine."

She was as nervous tonight as she'd been a year ago. But not about Paul. He'd turned out to be a very devoted and loving husband. The cast on his arm had been removed shortly after the accident and he didn't even have a scar. His job was demanding but he made up for it by dedicating himself to her whenever he was at home. She'd never met a man more content to just sit and enjoy the silence.

She'd been working on her fear of water and Paul had convinced her to spend Christmas on his yacht. They'd sailed from Cocoa down to Key West. Their time on the water had been special to her.

Corrine Martin, Paul's old secretary, had been promoted to a middle manager and had bid on and won Rand's services from Corporate Spouses. Kind of the same setup she and Paul had had. Angelica didn't allow her thoughts to dwell too long on Rand and Corrine, instead turned her attention to the podium.

"Lilly O'Malley is here representing Sleepy Time Nannies. The highest bidder will be awarded three months of nanny services and in-home instruction for first-time parents. We'll start the bidding tonight at five hundred dollars," said the auctioneer.

Angelica raised her hand to make her bid. She raised it three times before she won the nanny service.

"Congratulations, Mrs. Leone-Sterling, on winning," the emcee said.

"Angel, why did you bid on nanny services?" Paul asked when he returned.

"Because we'll be needing one."

"Adding a new service to Corporate Spouses?" he asked.

The man could still be a little dense at times. "Not my company. Us."

"Why do we…Angel, are you trying to tell me something?" he asked.

She nodded.

Paul pulled her to him and kissed her like a man who'd found life where he'd expected none. Kissed her like a man who'd been given a second chance. Kissed her like she was the key to his future. And she knew there was nothing they couldn't do together in life and in love.

*   *   *   *   *

Silhouette® Desire®

presents

DYNASTIES: THE CONNELLYS

A brand-new miniseries about the Connellys of Chicago,
a wealthy, powerful American family tied by blood to the
royal family of the island kingdom of Altaria.
They're wealthy, powerful and rocked by
scandal, betrayal...and passion!

Look for a whole year of glamorous and
utterly romantic tales in 2002:

January: **TALL, DARK & ROYAL** by Leanne Banks

February: **MATERNALLY YOURS** by Kathie DeNosky

March: **THE SHEIKH TAKES A BRIDE** by Caroline Cross

April: **THE SEAL'S SURRENDER** by Maureen Child

May: **PLAIN JANE & DOCTOR DAD** by Kate Little

June: **AND THE WINNER GETS...MARRIED!** by Metsy Hingle

July: **THE ROYAL & THE RUNAWAY BRIDE** by Kathryn Jensen

August: **HIS E-MAIL ORDER WIFE** by Kristi Gold

September: **THE SECRET BABY BOND** by Cindy Gerard

October: **CINDERELLA'S CONVENIENT HUSBAND**
by Katherine Garbera

November: **EXPECTING...AND IN DANGER** by Eileen Wilks

December: **CHEROKEE MARRIAGE DARE**
by Sheri WhiteFeather

Silhouette®
Where love comes alive™

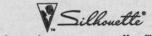

October 2002
TAMING THE OUTLAW
#1465 by Cindy Gerard

Don't miss bestselling author
Cindy Gerard's exciting story about
a sexy cowboy's reunion with his
old flame—and the daughter he
didn't know he had!

November 2002
ALL IN THE GAME
#1471 by Barbara Boswell

In the latest tale by beloved
Desire author Barbara Boswell,
a feisty beauty joins her twin as a
reality game show contestant in an
island paradise ...and comes face-to-
face with her teenage crush!

December 2002
A COWBOY & A GENTLEMAN
#1477 by Ann Major

Sparks fly when two fiery Texans are
brought together by matchmaking
relatives, in this dynamic story by
the ever-popular Ann Major.

MAN OF THE MONTH

Some men are made for lovin'—and you're sure to love
these three upcoming men of the month!

Available at your favorite retail outlet.

Where love comes alive™

Visit Silhouette at www.eHarlequin.com   SDMOM02Q4

If you enjoyed what you just read,
then we've got an offer you can't resist!

Take 2 bestselling love stories FREE!

Plus get a FREE surprise gift!

**Where royalty and romance
go hand in hand...**

The series finishes in

with these unforgettable love stories:

THE ROYAL TREATMENT
by Maureen Child
October 2002 (SD #1468)

TAMING THE PRINCE
by Elizabeth Bevarly
November 2002 (SD #1474)

ROYALLY PREGNANT
by Barbara McCauley
December 2002 (SD #1480)

COMING NEXT MONTH

#1465 TAMING THE OUTLAW—Cindy Gerard

After six years, sexy Cutter Reno was back in town and wreaking havoc on Peg Lathrop's emotions. Peg still yearned passionately for Cutter—and he wanted to pick up where they had left off. But would he still want her once he learned her precious secret?

#1466 CINDERELLA'S CONVENIENT HUSBAND—
Katherine Garbera
Dynasties: The Connellys

Lynn McCoy would do anything to keep the ranch that had been in her family for generations—even marry wealthy Seth Connelly. And when she fell in love with him, Lynn needed to convince her handsome husband they could have their very own happily-ever-after.

#1467 THE SEAL's SURPRISE BABY—Amy J. Fetzer

A trip home turned Jack Singer's life upside down because he learned that beautiful Melanie Patterson, with whom he'd spent one unforgettable night, had secretly borne him a daughter. The honor-bound Navy SEAL proposed a marriage of convenience. But Melanie refused, saying she didn't want him to feel obligated to her. Could Jack persuade her he wanted to be a *real* father…and husband?

#1468 THE ROYAL TREATMENT—Maureen Child
Crown and Glory

Determined to get an interview with the royal family, anchorwoman Jade Erickson went to the palace—and found herself trapped in an elevator in the arms of the handsomest man she'd ever seen. Jeremy Wainwright made her heart beat faster, and he was equally attracted to her, but would the flame of their unexpected passion continue to burn red-hot?

#1469 HEARTS ARE WILD—Laura Wright

Maggie Connor got more than she'd bargained for when she vowed to find the perfect woman for her very attractive male roommate. Nick Kaplan was turning out to be everything *she'd* ever wanted in a man, and she was soon yearning to keep him for herself!

#1470 SECRETS, LIES…AND PASSION—Linda Conrad

An old flame roared back to life when FBI agent Reid Sorrels returned to his hometown to track a suspect. His former fiancée, Jill Bennett, was as lovely as ever, and the electricity between them was undeniable. But they both had secrets.…

SDCNM0902